IMPOSSIBLE FIGURES

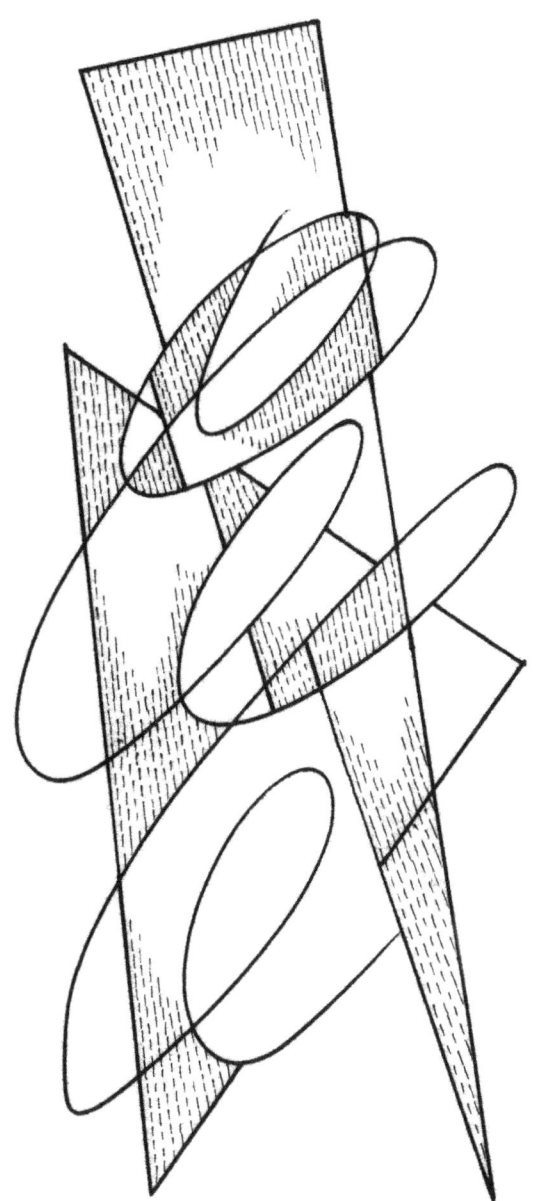

IMPOSSIBLE FIGURES

Novel/Art

Rick Moss

AERODYNE
PRESS

This book is a work of fiction. The characters, incidents, and dialogue are drawn from the author's imagination and are not to be construed as real. Any resemblance to actual events or persons, living or dead, is entirely coincidental.

Impossible Figures
Copyright © 2020 by Rick Moss

impossiblefigures.com

For information and ordering:
Aerodyne Press
PO Box 150546
Brooklyn, NY 11215
info@aerodynepress.com

ISBN: 978-0-9831666-4-1

For Janet

"Art for me is the science of freedom."

– Joseph Beuys

"Both art and science in their own ways advance by rejecting old truths and establishing new truths. Try to integrate the two unaligned efforts and you basically fuck yourself silly."

– Oscar Hiller

CHAPTER ONE

In which Ranger, a conceptual artist and subject of a quantum state experiment, witnesses a version of the death of Oscar Hiller, a student of the physical sciences.

"Oscar, are you awake?"

In the near darkness, Ranger reached out a finger and traced the curve of Oscar's cheekbone without making contact.

The van was quiet, save for Oscar's phlegmy breaths. Outside, traffic passed on the boulevard a block up the hill.

"You will wake soon, Oscar. Seems longer, this one," Ranger said. "Seems like a longer wait, but it should be the same—roughly the same."

Ranger raised his eyes to the salt-dusted windshield, lit by a distant street lamp. "I would like to talk, Oscar. It would be nice to talk for a bit before they get here."

He arched his back and expanded his chest, as if filling his lungs with the frigid air. He mimicked the act of blowing.

"No cloud." He waved his hand through the space where a cloud would be illuminated by the gray light.

Curled on the ribbed metal floor before Ranger, Oscar lay bundled head to shoes in a dank moving blanket, stiffened like plaster in the single-digit cold.

Ranger was naked and semitransparent. He sat cross-legged by Oscar and to some degree intersected the space occupied by a rusty gas can wedged behind the driver's seat.

Two young men could now be heard approaching, the staccato beats of their argument, the slip-crunch of their boots on the ice as they made their way down the steep side street.

A moment later the footsteps came to a halt just outside.

"It was you who did her, you squirmy fuck," said one.

Ranger shook his head at the frantic boot shuffling that followed, the verbal lashes and the pounding of elbows and skulls against the outside of the van.

Oscar stirred and huffed. He choked and moaned in complaint in the way an engine might resist turning over on a cold night.

"Yes, Oscar," said Ranger, "there you are. Wake up, friend. Do you hear them out there, Oscar? Can you hear the fight underway?"

Oscar's eye cracked open. It drifted closed.

"Oscar, we haven't much time. Listen, earlier at the party, you were taken by the Escher drawing."

The quarrel heated up outside. "Tell me, you shit-scum! You were with her. Tell me."

Oscar jolted awake with a thud on the side of the van.

"Look at me," said Ranger. He snapped his fingers, but they emitted no sound. "Can you see me, Oscar? This version of tonight is going more quickly. It would be nice to chat."

Oscar made an effort to shake the blanket from his face. He forced his eyes wide on Ranger. "Heesh. It's a Viking. Your'n— You're not really all there. I'm—shit, I'm all—"

"I'm not fully here, no. I thought you might tell me why I'm in this odd state. Do you remember the Escher drawing? Think. Maybe that will help orient you."

Oscar smiled and closed his eyes. "Feer flucking weird. I'm not here too—either."

"You are very much here, Oscar. You're very drunk. Try to picture the Escher drawing. It may lead your thinking to my situation, to the different versions of tonight."

Oscar burped out a laugh, bringing on a horrid cough. He freed enough of his head to raise it a few degrees. "Did I fall asleep?" He twisted his chin toward the front seat. "Wait, who drunk me— Who put me back here? Did I drive?"

"No, Oscar, you made no attempt to drive. It was your friend, the blond one, about your height. About your everything, actually. Why have I forgotten his name? He always helps you into the van, wraps you in that filthy blanket. He drives you here, and then goes into the bar."

"Tookie?"

"Yes, of course—Tookie. So odd I can't remember. It must be an anomaly of, well, what's happened to me. But please, Oscar, the Escher drawing was—"

"Escher. What? The artist guy? No."

"Listen, Oscar, you're almost out of time, and I'm curious to know how—"

"Wuh, slow down, man of the—Norse." Oscar pawed at his face. "I can't feel shit. Am I touching myself?"

The floor rocked. The combatants were wrestling against the side of the van. "Micky! Shit," said the other. "Stop. Enough, man. Don't!"

"That's Tookie. Tookie!" Oscar forced his head up but failed to move anything else.

"Don't mind them," said Ranger. "Look, look here. Eyes on me. Escher's staircase fascinated you. What did you call it? A Penrose triangle, am I right?"

Oscar let his head drop back. "Penrose— What the hell did I drink? This some kind of drunk. And you're damn Viking ghosty-ghost."

A screech outside, and the van resounded with clanging, metal-on-metal.

"Enough of that, damn it," said Oscar. "Who's hitting my van? I—"

"Please, can we focus on the Penrose triangle, Oscar?"

"That's Tookie out there. Is somebody hitting Tookie?" Oscar propped up onto an elbow, but again he was unsuccessful and fell back.

"You took drugs as well, Oscar. I couldn't say what kind."

Oscar grimaced. "Oh fuck me, the Nembutal. Phoenie's Nembutal."

"And you stopped shivering at least an hour ago, so you're likely in an advanced stage of hypothermia. It's shy of five degrees in here."

Oscar was staring through Ranger to the location of impact on the van wall.

"Oscar, look at me." Ranger wiggled his fingers. "That's Micky out there. He's beating Tookie. Micky is beating Tookie to death, and he'll soon be—"

"No, come on. Help me. I can't feel my—" Oscar jerked his head away from Ranger but failed to roll over.

"It's no use, Oscar. Your extremities are frozen. And in any case, you don't have long to live—a few minutes at best. That considered, can we please just talk about this strange state I'm in because—"

"Who the— I don't know you. I don't give a shit about—"

"Yes, you do. I'm Ranger. I'm the artist you met at the party. Try to remember."

"Just get me up, damn you. Help me get up."

"I wish I could, Oscar. I can't, physically speaking, because I'm not fully present."

A key scratched at the back door in search of the ice-coated lock.

"Why does he always assume the door is locked?" Ranger said.

The back door creaked open revealing the killer's dark form. As he stepped aside, the van brightened with the street light.

Ranger rose to a crouch beside Oscar. "I'm sorry, my friend," he said. "You should cover up. Hide yourself. Time for me to go."

"Wait, no. Please don't. Is that Micky? He's going to—"

"You don't want Micky to find you, not in his present condition, not that it seems to matter. You're dying in nearly every version, regardless of your actions. You're bound to—"

Outside, Micky was sobbing.

"Oh, I've dawdled," said Ranger, "and now I'm stuck witnessing this. It's so disconcerting, witnessing this."

Micky's footfalls returned. Oscar flapped his numb forearms and succeeded in repositioning the blanket over his face. He lay back, wheezing from the effort.

The interior light waned as the killer reappeared in the doorway with Tookie's rubbery body draped over his shoulder. Steam rose from Micky's bare arms and billowed out with each breath. He bent his knees and, with a whimper, flipped the body forward through the doorway.

Tookie uncoiled like an unbound mattress onto the van floor, his head thudding against Oscar's hip. Strands of Tookie's long hair draped as thick as liquorish with half-frozen blood.

Oscar lay still. Micky tossed the tire iron inside and slammed the door. As his footsteps rounded the side, Ranger slipped from the passenger's seat back into the shadows by Oscar.

"Oscar," he said, "You'll use the tire iron. In other versions, the tire iron seems like it may be offering you a chance."

"What? No, this is crazy," said Oscar, from underneath. "What versions? Please."

"Not crazy, no—baffling. I do find it frustrating."

The driver's door opened.

Ranger hunkered down behind the seat.

He whispered to Oscar. "The tire iron."

Micky Green, feet still on the ground, reached inside and gripped the wheel. He let his head sag for a long moment, then pulled himself onto the driver's seat. "I can't. Oh my God." He shook the wheel.

He smacked his ears with open palms. He punched the dashboard and threw his shoulders back, nearly knocking the seat off its runners.

After some time, Micky quieted. He removed his knit cap and used it to clear the steamed windshield.

He started the van.

The motor chugged and died. Micky cried out like a shamed child. He stamped the gas three times and restarted.

Micky gunned the engine and threw the gear shift into drive. The van lurched off. He yanked the wheel left into a fishtailing U-turn up the hill toward Main.

Behind, Oscar was sent rolling toward the passenger's side. Half loosed from the blanket, he landed stomach-down over the tire iron. Micky glanced over his shoulder at the kettle-drum beats of the gas can tumbling diagonally into the rear door.

Gas odor filled the interior.

Micky accelerated through the stop sign at the corner and veered wide onto Main Street. A cab driver in the oncoming lane sounded his horn and swerved too late to avoid a smack on his left rear panel.

Micky, corrected for the rebound, then punched the gas, passing back over the double yellow.

He wrenched at his left ear, as if removing it would ease his pain. He slalomed through traffic, eyes forward as he passed derelict used car lots and darkened print shops and sandwich joints.

Micky tore through town without tapping the break, then entered a broad intersection blocked by a laundry van and a lineup of cars waiting to turn. He threw the wheel right. The tires skipped over a ridge of sloppily plowed ice, sending the van's tail winging into rotation.

Micky applied more gas and wiggled back on course. He cut left at the next corner for a shortcut to Route 9.

Ranger lay on his side by Oscar. "He's managed to stay on the road longer than other versions," he whispered in Oscar's ear. "Your body should be warming some, Oscar. You should get ready to make your move."

Oscar shifted his arms under him, scraping the tire iron against the van floor.

Micky twitched in the direction of the noise but was midway through his turn onto the state highway. He cut off a semi coming on at full speed. The trucker lay on his horn and loomed over the van's rear bumper. Micky jogged the van away into the far left lane and floored it, spitting out a brown spray from the berm of snow stacked against the Jersey barrier.

Micky sobbed. "You fucking loser. You're a fucking nothing. You threw it away." He beat his head against his window.

"You have no choice, Oscar," Ranger whispered. "There's a complicated junction ahead. He'll never make it through. You have to stop him now."

Oscar pushed up with his elbows. He kept his head down and sat back on his heels, groping for the tire iron with his numb hands.

Micky rolled out belly moans and coughed from the thickening gas fumes.

Oscar worked his fingers under the bar and hugged it into the crook of his elbows. He sucked in a breath as he rose and got a lungful of gas vapor.

Oscar hacked.

Micky turned to see and allowed the van to drift left into a tumble of snow boulders. The front tire hopped off the berm, pivoting the van clockwise until the rear left bumper ground against the concrete barrier. Micky clenched the wheel and slammed the brake.

Oscar, thrown forward into the front cab, bounded off the edge of the passenger seat and fell toward Micky. The spear end of the tire iron glanced off Micky's temple and tore into the bridge of his nose.

Micky flailed. His right wrist caught the wheel and twirled it left.

The van climbed the berm and launched. The motor revved once and died, leaving only the whine of the rear wheels, like distant drills.

Ranger sung out in a matching pitch. "Oh, it's happening now. Again and again it's happening now."

As the van barrel-rolled over the barrier, Oscar flipped rearward, for a moment suspended in the same space occupied by Ranger. Then, just as he might have regained contact with solid matter, Oscar was dispersed by the gas explosion, bringing his elements in a different sense into union with those of his friends, Tookie and Micky Green.

CHAPTER TWO

We learn of the events leading up to another version of Oscar's death, and of the killer, Micky Green, and his grand revelation: that humans are instruments through which the universe strives to become self-aware.

Late one early December afternoon, Oscar was slapping his way up lower Main Street in his treadless Keds, eyes stinging from the whipping sleet, when he came upon the forlorn downtown VA Hall. He paused and checked over his shoulder. Absent an oncoming municipal bus, he took refuge inside.

Oscar opened the vestibule door onto the Hall, its broad floor vacant but for two threadbare billiard tables. Across the room, two lone drinkers anchored one end of a thirty-foot bar. Micky Green had one ass cheek on the bar stool, one foot on the floor, bending in over a rheumy, slack-eyed vet who, though clearly uncomprehending, sputtered the occasional laugh, no doubt hopeful of getting in on Micky's next round.

Micky's Samson curls bobbled as he spoke. His ropey arms, swept and splayed. At a point, he noticed the new arrival and waved him in.

Once within reach, Micky pulled Oscar close. "Your first time, right? You served in Laos or some shit. Just say Laos. These old pud grippers don't know dick about Laos."

"Was the U.S. in Laos?" said Oscar.

"Hard to say, man. Hard to say."

Buzz, the bartender, positioned at far end of the counter, was snipping at the innards of an old watch with a needle nose pliers. At the squeak of Oscar's stool legs on the linoleum, he flipped his jeweler's glass onto his forehead and hobbled over, his empty sleeve flapping in rhythm to his lopsided gait.

"Where'd he serve?" he said, pointing at Oscar.

"Delta Province," Oscar said. He pulled his sweater up to mop the slush from his brow.

"When?"

"Too damn long, that's when. What's it matter? I didn't come in to tell stories."

The bartender nodded. He popped the cap off a long-neck and brought it to Oscar. "First one's on the hall." He pointed to Micky's empty Mr. Pibb bottle. "Another?"

Micky pinged his bottle with his fingernail. Once Buzz had turned, Micky laid his cheek on the bar and grinned up at Oscar.

Oscar tilted his bottle toward him. "Figured there's always a Delta Province," he said.

Micky hooked an elbow around Oscar's neck. "Oh, yeah, you're gifted, man. One look at you, shit—Delta Province." Micky sang, "The sound of a man fit for being in the shit," popping Oscar in the chest. "Bum-da-bum-bum. Soldier boy music. And you knew, didn't you? You knew just what Buzz was waiting on. He was waiting on that sweet little bugle line. Del-ta Pro-vince."

They cooled it while Buzz replaced Micky's bottle.

"Preconceptions," said Oscar, as soon as Buzz was out of earshot.

Micky grabbed Oscar by the ears and shook. "Preconceptions. You're a musician, man. And I mean that in a higher sense. Me too. We can hear those tunes. And woe be on them who can't, those sad mothers, 'cause them who can't sing are just, I don't know—absorbing. They're egg crates, deadening sound. Do what you do, man. Sing your tune. You don't want to be on the absorbing end. You want to be the bugle. Preconceptions? Hell, yeah. What's your name? You in school? You go to Scummler U.? You a Scummie?"

It went on this way for some time, Micky going at Oscar like he was pounding seeds to extract kernels.

"You know, man," said Micky wiggling fingers above his head for another round, "perception-wise, as I was saying, your majority of mobility-endowed assholes are at best just absorbing and echoing. Aren't more than a handful like us around who can really hear— and see. You see what I'm saying? You do. You do. I grew up here and I'm telling you, all the see'ers in this town wouldn't fill these bar stools. And us see'ers, we're the ones calling what's real real. Those other sorry mothers are waiting for us to do the seeing for them, right? We're accountable for deciding what's fucking real. Without us, they're in a dead-end fucking state because, without us, there's no real."

Oscar paused his bottle an inch from his lips. "You're talking quantum perception."

"Wow. Yeah? Explain, explain, explain."

"Jeez." Oscar raised his eyes to the ceiling and swigged. "This should be fun."

Oscar stretched down the bar and grabbed a discarded lemon wedge. He placed it in front of Micky. "Ok, here it is."

"Lemon."

"We, you know, people," said Oscar, "sense the world through, well, our senses—eyes, nose, so forth. What is actually happening is we're picking up waves—pulses in wave form, pulsing along these polarized neural axons. Whatever. The thing is, our sense organs funnel waves into our brains and from those we somehow make sense of the world. You might think, well, I'm looking at a lemon wedge. You think, light's bouncing off this lemon wedge and the lemon-light passes through my eyes, and my eyes are lenses, right, and they project the lemon image onto my brain like a projector on a movie screen."

Micky nodded. He flicked the lemon wedge for a twirl on the bar, and nodded some more.

"Well, it's nothing like that," said Oscar. "Your brain's got nothing but wave data to go on. And those waves stay fucking waves until the brain says to itself, these waves are telling me to create a lemon wedge perception. Without the brain, no lemon wedge, just fucking waves."

Micky was frozen.

Oscar polished off his beer.

"The observer does the creating," Oscar said. "The observer doesn't see a lemon wedge, he creates a perception of the fucking lemon wedge."

Micky jolted upright like an ice cube had been dropped down his collar. "Oh, well hell, man. We're God."

Oscar chuckled. "Hardly."

"No, no," said Micky, "what I'm saying is, there's no God-god like they teach you, but we're really God because we're the Creator. These numb-nuts say God sees everything—knows all, sees all. They've got the whole universe bastard-ackwards. The universe—it, man—is seeing through us because we see things and—"

"Because we define what's real."

"Right," said Micky. "Right. But more, more, more—we are the Creator. We're the see-er for the universe because the universe, like you're saying, is just fucking waves wiggling every which fucking way. It's just acting the way it's gotta act. It's dancing to the only rhythm it can. It doesn't know why it dances. It doesn't know anything. Wind doesn't know why it blows, grass doesn't know why it grows."

"Just one, big idiot universe."

"But I'll tell you something, man." Micky gripped Oscar by the shoulder. "The universe, it will someday assume the God position. Someday the universe will come to fucking know why it dances. And then, well, well—"

"What?"

"Well, universe-God happens."

"When it's self-aware."

"Right, right, right, right. And you know it's inevitable because—shit, what do you call it? Being self-aware, that's what it's always been after."

"Evolutionary imperative."

Micky beamed. He gave Oscar's cheek five little slaps.

"Shit, quit it." Oscar waved Buzz in for another round.

"No, no, you gotta know it, man," Micky said. "All that the universe has ever done leading up 'til now—this gazillion-year plan to evolve a damn slimy microbe into a mollusk into a monkey into these bizarrely big-brained bastards who can make waves into lemon-wedges—that, my friend, is the whole fucking universe, all of creation, wanting to see, wanting to know, man. It's the universe with a deep-body yearning to create a beast that it can see through—know through—so it can once and for all understand what the fuck itself is. And once the universe comes to know itself, well—fuck, I don't know what."

"It'll roll over, kick the whore out of bed, and start a new day," said Oscar. He lifted a new bottle to his lips.

Micky screeched like a falcon. He hopped up on his barstool and raised his arms like he had conquered a summit.

"That, you royal numb-nut motherfuckers of New England is what every stinking thing in your overfed, color-blind, directionless lives is about," Micky sang. "That's why we're here. That's what painting and pinball and symphonies and soft-serve cones and everything that every sorry, misguided loser on earth has ever done to raise himself above the beasts is all about. It's about the universe evolving us into what it needs us to be so it can open its cosmic eyes through us and become God. Through us, man! The universe is becoming aware through us."

Oscar scratched at the back of his neck.

Micky lowered his arms. "What, man? What're you thinking? I'm right, right? What're you thinking? Hey, what'd you say your name was? You're a Scummie, I bet, but not your average Scummie, right? I saw you on campus, I think, right?"

Oscar checked the clock under the Genesee bar light. "My van's getting a new radiator and I've got to work the dinner shift in fifteen minutes. Do you have a car?"

They rode to campus in Micky's rattletrap '74 Karmann Ghia. Micky drove with abandon, like he talked.

On the short drive, Oscar learned that, despite appearances, Micky was not a genuine townie, having spent his adolescence in a respectable housing development on the outskirts of the old industrial berg. His dad, Otz, moved them there when he saw that the only education Micky and his thick-skulled brothers were receiving was on the city streets.

The new split-level was all their long-suffering mom ever wanted.

"I got the feeling once Mom settled into 'burbia she saw she'd got as good as she was going to get," said Micky. Within two years, his mother succumbed to cervical cancer. "It was like she cashed in her chips for two fucking years of happy."

Otz's temperament didn't change when his wife died. He was a calloused blue collar Jew who went from factory grunt to feared businessman in an instant, seizing an opportunity in a fashion ruthless enough to ward off possible competition for decades.

Otz parented with physical instruction, not for love of cruelty, but for the sake of expediency. The corrective whacks worked on his brothers but only sent Micky careering off in deviant trajectories.

"I don't know shit about what my dad went through when he was a kid except what was implied by his knuckles." Micky's hands were all over the wheel as he veered around the parked cars on the ice-impeded streets. "I got a lesson with every fucking smack saying, 'Don't rely on anybody. Don't regret anything.'"

Oscar shielded his face with his elbows as the Ghia launched off a mound of snow and bottomed out upon landing.

"My old man, you gotta picture him," said Micky, "can tear down a printing press with a couple of tools and rebuild the bastard in the dark. He's a hard-ass SOB and he always knew by gut how to go for whatever he was after.

"He's got business tied up all over town—got his maintenance crews now in half the plants. That doesn't happen unless you know which particular heads to bust open."

Oscar nodded, glued to the blurred action passing by outside.

"See these wrists?"

Oscar allowed himself a glance.

"Big fucking joints—machine joints. I got these from my old man.

Look at these big, knobs I got for shoulders. Ever seen a rag joint?"

Oscar shook his head.

"Here's what I remember about being a little kid," he said, maintaining speed. "I'm riding with the bastard in his panel truck. There's no passenger seat, so I'm sitting on a crate full of greasy machine parts. We're knocking along up and down these hills, winter potholes tossing me up in the air—me and the cotter pins and wing nuts. My dad doesn't say shit. He likes it to be a shock to the system when he tells you something. The truck's insides are lined floor to ceiling with every goddamn kinda tool—socket sets clattering so loud, it's not like you could talk anyway. Half the day, it's me bouncing like a little jerk thinking about God knows what. Him thinking of God knows what, the bastard. That was childhood."

Micky swung right off of Main Street onto a narrow campus road, restricted to campus police.

On his break that night, Oscar went out to the loading dock to smoke with Tookie. The two, bouncing to keep feeling alive in their toes, could have passed for brothers, though Tookie was an inch taller and a shade blonder. Of the non-student full-timers at the dining hall, Tookie was the only one interested in what Oscar had to say.

Tookie was townie through and through, complete with a tribal, comic book nickname. The others in the crew—Paunch, Rut Rut, Fleazy, Butterball—had earned their titles via childhood accomplishments, whether heroic or humiliating. But Tookie was dubbed earlier in life by his Swedish grandmother, something to do with his baby fat. He was also by far the sharpest of the bunch.

Oscar asked Tookie if he had ever encountered Micky Green.

Tookie exhaled out the side of his mouth, waving to dispel the smoke. "Encounter. Good word for Micky. We're tight, which is what you're wanting to be, Micky-wise, or staying clear. So Micky's out of rehab. Damn. I'd expect to've heard from him by now."

Tookie authenticated Micky's portrayal of Otz. He had witnessed a couple of disciplinary episodes. "You watch Micky keep his feet planted whilst getting belt-whipped 'cross the ear by Otz and you know what he's made of, man. You know what they're both fucking made of."

Turns out in the aftermath of one such incident, Micky convinced a chop shop to give him sixteen-hundred for Otz's prized Buick sedan. He put down three months on a room in a clapboard house in town, adopted a stray Rottweiler mix, and applied himself to getting in deep with some lowlife townies.

Micky's relationships were never anything but all-in, and being all-in with these particular fools led to a serious smack habit. One afternoon, after getting an update on his condition (Tookie may have played a role), Otz paid his son a visit. He found the tenement floor tiled with pancaked dog shit and Micky about twenty pounds shy of his high school wrestling weight. He dragged Micky out to Fitchburg for treatment.

"Never saw anybody take to drugs so fast and so endearing as Micky Green," said Tookie.

Three days later at closing time, Oscar passed through the quad as Micky arrived to meet up with Tookie and crew. Oscar was sucked into Micky's orbit and dragged along for the evening's activities. In the weeks that followed, with Micky's endorsement, the guys drew Oscar into the fold.

Most nights commenced with a manic tour of the town in the Karmann Ghia. With three stuffed in back and one across their laps, five could ride along. As a matter of pride, Micky took every turn at full speed and favored flooring it on the downhill, especially if a red traffic light beckoned at the bottom. Micky would graze the brake once or twice to instill a speck of hope, then for the last twenty yards bear down on the accelerator. Safely through on one occasion, Oscar reopened his eyes to discover Fleazy absent from the front seat, somehow tucked beneath the dash.

In lieu of a kegger, McGonigel's was the go-to bar due to its close proximity to campus and the opportunity to goof on the Scummies. Micky et al would cast their shadows over a booth and displace the thin-bearded freshman, polishing off their abandoned pitchers.

Any conversation involving Micky became the Micky Show. When not dominating, he disrupted. Like a tree obstructing a rapid current, he would send plumes of verbiage skyward.

One slow Wednesday night, Paunch and Rut Rut were at each other about their respective sisters. Micky wasn't satisfied with the caliber of discourse. "You gonna take that, Paunch? He just made your sister out to be, well, like your mother, and we all know what she's like."

If the group encountered a lull, Micky would prod around for a tender spot.

"Fleazy, aren't you the Aerosmith fan?"

"I like Dream On. Not sure about—"

"Oh, damn, well who wouldn't? Dream On's a classic. When Steve whatshisname crosses his legs and gets his voice up real high and girly, any guy's gonna feel his scrotals going all prickly-pear, am I right? That's just natural."

"It's not like it's my favorite or—"

"No doubt, Fleaze, you find his look irresistible—long and lean and agile. He's— What's that word, Oscar?"

"Svelte."

"Svelte, yeah. And, heck, you're a dream on kind of guy, Fleaz, being you've never properly had a woman and such, and I'd wager you're—"

"Hey, fuck you man, I had more than—"

"But wait, no, there was that lesbian chick. What was her name? Bernard? Her name's Bernard, right? Did she locate your erogenous zones, Fleazy? She bring you along nice and gentle?"

"Beatrice. She's bi. She's not—"

"I'd wager what she brought along was a manly device of some sort. And I'm not disparaging gay people. Some of my favorite people are gay people, like your dad and your Uncle Shiny."

"Hey, fucking watch it, Micky. F'you think I'm gonna—"

"Wait, I actually never met your Uncle Shiny. Maybe you were making reference to your dad's man-part. But Bernard, shit, it's gotta confuse your natural tendencies to be with a mannish woman who would rather be with a womanly female than a furry-ass guy like you, unless you could somehow provide the feminine aspect she was after."

Fleazy had a foot up on the bench in preparation to launch across the table at Micky. Tookie took hold of his scarf like a leash.

The bartender came over to break things up. Oscar scooted laterally to join a table of Scummler women. Lakshmi, the TA from his previous semester's Quantum Phys 131 class, was present.

Micky leaned back on his bench to enjoy the interplay between the bartender, Paunch, and Fleazy, stretching his legs out into the aisle. Besides inheriting Otz's joints, Micky was heir to his father's lankiness. He had flowing black hair, blocky cheekbones and lips full enough to ingratiate him on the African continent.

Lakshmi asked Oscar for an introduction, but when he tried to wave him over, Micky tipped an imaginary hat and ducked out toward another table in the back.

"If I didn't know better," Oscar said to Tookie later as they walked home, "I'd say Micky is scared of women."

"Not women, just Phoenicia. You met her? Not sure if they're on or off this week."

"Not yet."

"A match made in the lower depths. You know how Micky draws trouble? Well, Phoenie's drawn to it. She worships trouble in all styles and colors."

As Tookie figured it, Micky seemed unable to live without acting up, but he suffered in the aftermath of his destructive episodes. Phoenicia was unrepentant.

"The possibility of screwing with Micky makes her get all creative inside. She gets sexed up. I seen her rag on him like she's racking up points at pinball."

"Micky tolerates that?"

"It's painful to see. Micky's in awe of Phoenie."

Micky was also foolish enough, said Tookie, to confide in Phoenicia. Micky told her one night in post-coital openness how, when barely pubescent, an assistant coach had solicited him with a suggestion for the proper use of his oversized lips, and what followed tortured Micky like an untreated wound. Rut Rut had a notch out of his left ear attesting to his poor judgment in laughing when Micky entrusted him with the story.

"Phoenie'll tell lip jokes about Micky the second he leaves the room," said Tookie. "She's a real pissah, Phoenie is."

Oscar walked to campus one frigid Saturday to work the dinner shift. He shook off the cold as he made his way through the student lounge and climbed the open stairs to the dining hall on the second level. The kitchen was a humid fifteen degrees warmer than the rest of the building and hushed during the break save for an occasional indicator beep or steam hiss. He found the full-time crew huddled in the dish washing room. They smiled at him in unison.

"You got training on the deep fryer, right Oscar?" said Paunch, eliciting giggles from the group.

"Why?" Oscar said.

"Yup, he was," said Tookie. They laughed.

"OK, what's up?" Oscar tried again.

"Nothing, man," said Fleazy. "Just that tonight's Elephant Toenails, so somebody's gonna get fryer duty, which being that it's a badge of honor you'd say and it could be you which it could be a real feather in your cap were you the volunteer when old Inge asks who wants to volunteer."

"Thanks for the tip," said Oscar.

Inge was the head chef, a sweet, hair-netted little potato dumpling who wielded her battle-ax as necessary to keep the diabolical crew of young punks in line.

Oscar, as a student, had experienced the anarchy of Elephant Toenail night. The Scummies stormed the food line to win double helpings of Inge's chicken parm patties, which she had taught the crew to lay out in baking pans in military rows, slather with her doctored Hunt's tomato sauce, and top with a half moon each of processed provolone (hence the toenail reference). The Scummies couldn't get enough.

Inge soon arrived for the shift with her cadre of chefs and gathered the boys by the prep tables to set the night's assignments. Oscar piped up before Inge started, vying to run the massive conveyor dishwasher. Inge approved, drawing sighs of disappointment from the others.

"OK, OK, I know vhat you boys are up to so stop mit zee foolishness tonight, you hear me? I have not a bit of patience. Paunchy, you do the fryer, sweetheart."

Tookie snickered.

"And you, Mr. Tookie, you vatch yourself, young man. No cubing, you hear? A cubing and I'll can you lickety-schplit."

Oscar, besides avoiding whatever mischief was underfoot, enjoyed the solitude of the dishwasher room. When graced with the duty, he took extra time flushing out the machine's inner recesses and food traps with the pressure hose, polishing the stainless steel surfaces, and monitoring the temperature settings so the gauges were in ideal positions when Inge checked in.

While the cooks and assistants prepped, Oscar cranked up the Hobart to sanitizing temperature, set up the night's supply of flatware, glasses, and dishes in neat stacks for the runners, and rolled open the tray return window. His student help didn't arrive until an hour into service time, so he drifted out to the prep line to kill ten minutes.

Inge and her cooks, Maria and Lily, who gave the impression they were raised in the same village in the old country, gossiped away in Bavarian while scaling the step ladders to dump multi-gallon cans of ingredients into the five foot diameter soup kettles.

Oscar brought the ladies a round of Frescas from the dispenser out front and then headed to the back line to check out the guys. Tookie was up to his elbows in grease cutter suds at the pot scrubbing station. Paunch was across the aisle and down the way ten feet, lowering the fifth and sixth of eight basketfuls into the deep fryer. The frozen chicken patties hissed and spit and then churned up waves of boiling oil nearly overflowing the fryer bath.

Paunch was wearing a wool Bruins ski mask and a pair of safety goggles that were opaque with steam and grease splatters. The ambient temperature at the station was roughly 125 degrees. Paunch, who was six-two and a full bodied guy, had sweated through his kitchen whites from neck to knees.

Tookie pivoted to place a clean baking sheet into the drying rack and caught Oscar's eye with a wink. He shuffled back to his sink as Inge made a pass through.

Inge paused by the deep fryer station. "Randall, my Got—I mean to say, Paunchy—vhat in the earth you tinking, Paunchy? You take that ting off of you right now and put on proper kitchen cap. My Got, vhat on earth?"

Paunchy complied, revealing a rotund face a shade of red no face should be, and drenched hair matted into a spiral.

Inge patted Oscar on the shoulder. "Sweetie, please, you get Randall some cool orangeade before he collapse. My Got, these boys."

Tookie whispered as Oscar passed on his way to the dispenser. "Pssst. Cup of ice, dude. Cup of ice, man."

Oscar returned. Tookie took his ice cup and slipped it out of sight.

Oscar continued on and handed Paunch his drink. The big guy stepped back from the fryer, mopped his face with a soiled dishtowel, and downed the orangeade. He stood eyeing the pot scrubber station until Tookie looked his way. Paunch lifted a middle finger and then shook a fist at him.

Tookie pantomimed a response one might see from an electro-shock therapy patient. Paunch advanced toward him, but then turned back to answer the beeping fry timer.

Oscar was on his way back to the dish room when the clatter of cascading furniture broke from the dining hall followed by cries of distress. As Inge and the cooks passed out of the kitchen through the swinging doors, he caught a glimpse of Fleazy lying under a pile of chairs that had been stacked on the side to make room for mopping.

Oscar smiled and hurried back to the fryer area in time to catch Tookie trotting past the fryer station and hooking an ice cube over Paunch's right shoulder into the boiling fryer bath.

The exploding cube gave off a vicious mouse trap snap. Paunch shrieked at a pitch inconceivable for a person his size. He bounced on tip-toes and gyrated, batting at the fiery grease dotting his face and arms.

Tookie broke into a sprint, circumnavigated the kitchen and made it back to his sink before the ladies returned. Oscar watched him for a few moments until he spotted Tookie's knees buckling from suppressed laughter.

Oscar soaked a clean towel in ice water and draped it over Paunch's head, then took sanctuary in his dish room in time to greet the night's student workers.

At the conclusion of the shift, Oscar hosed down his room, squeegeed all surfaces, and backed his way out of the dish room door with the completion of his mopping pattern. By then, it was half past seven. Tookie had long since cleaned his area and was hanging out with the other guys in the atrium of the student union.

Anyone passing through would have thought the workers were students. Most of the townies were stringy-haired white guys who smoked a lot, indistinguishable from a prevalent element among the student body, except that the townies bought their clothes at the discount barn out on Route 9 and the students bought theirs at an overpriced local secondhand store. Townies, in fact, were sometimes known to demand their discarded flannel shirts and baseball jackets back from Scummies.

With Tookie's appearance, a volley of taunts, threats, and laudation echoed through the poured concrete modernist structure. Tookie let Paunch chase him around an oversized ottoman, then grabbed Oscar by the shoulders and used him as a human shield.

Oscar broke free and cut toward the side exit. "I'm outta here," he said. "Catch you up at McG's."

Micky arrived soon thereafter in a twitchy mood. He was soon followed by Gordie Dremkarski, a campus cop related in some way to three of the townies present. Gordie asked them to take the rough-housing off-site and, when that failed, pleaded for pity given that he was still on probation for turning a blind eye to an unnamed group that two months prior stole a monstrous wooden cable spool from a construction area on campus and rolled it into traffic on Main Street.

After torturing Gordie for a time, the group exited, but being that the temperature had plunged below ten degrees, dispersed in short order. Micky latched onto Tookie, and Paunch tagged along, still in a pout, but much calmed.

Micky drove with uncharacteristic deliberation, equivocating at corners and keeping the speed at near legal. Ultimately, he turned onto Walnut Street, slowing as he approached Phoenicia's block.

"You back with Phoenie?" said Tookie.

Micky rubbed at his ear. He rolled down the window to spit. "Sure, sure. Let's pick Phoenie up. She might be, well, yeah."

Paunch relinquished his seat to Phoenie and stuffed himself in the back with Tookie. Most of the air in the tiny car was thereby displaced, and what was left was soon thick with the output of Phoenie's Kools.

Micky snaked block by block around the Jesuit college nearby. Phoenie twirled the radio knobs for a while, hissing back at the static. She clicked the radio off and the car went quiet.

"I think you missed a street," said Tookie, after a bit when Micky abandoned the neighborhood.

"Dry over here tonight, but I'll sniff one out near Scummler."

Phoenie was nail-tapping at high frequency on the passenger window and cracking her gum in syncopation.

"The reception in this town sucks," said Micky. "I'm looking into a tape deck."

"Yeah, you're lookin' for shit. If you can't get music workin' in this shit can, you can't call the fucker a car. And what do you think I want to drink from a Scummie keg for anyway? Like I'd wrap my lips 'round a Scummie tap."

Micky's head was low and angled. "No mystery what's got you like this, Phoenie. I could see your fangs showing the second you got in. I told you don't be on that bitch-on-wheels crystal around me."

"Oh, here he comes with the ex-junky lecture. We'll call you Mr. Clean for a Day 'cause that's about how long you'll last."

"And sure enough, Phoenie, first time we're together since before Thanksgiving and— What is it, anyway? Angel dust? Nah, usually dust just makes you twinkly. What they cut it with?"

"Oh, I forgot, skag freaks got like a sixth sense for getting all envious when it comes to others having a little fun. Well, I ain't on no crystal, Micky, so maybe you need more drug practice."

"Great advice. That's just the kind of support a guy needs, coming out of rehab. Maybe you'd like to blow that fairy dust of yours at me for good measure because I'm not quite totally enabled yet."

Phoenie leaned in close. "Hey, lover, speaking of fairies, maybe we should hit that Scummie party after all. I'll get one of those Izod-wearing pretty boys to do me. I'm sure he'd be twice the fun you are."

Micky pulled the argument over to the curb outside a packies on upper Main Street. The couple kept at it until Micky jumped out to confront a threesome of jock types admiring his Ghia. He smacked a can of Bud out of one guy's hand, then wrenched the other to his knees by the collar. He turned back to the car before the students had a chance to pick themselves up, anxious to continue his last thought with Phoenie.

Phoenie started punctuating her gibes with two finger jabs into Micky's clavicle, then muted him with one just below his Adam's Apple.

She stepped out onto the curb. "I ain't fucked up, dickhead, not yet anyway. I'm going in there for a nice pint of Beam to take the edge off this dust you think I got the money for which I don't 'cause my skaggy-ass boyfriend is piss poor."

She took three steps toward the liquor store, then returned and reinserted her head.

"And by the way, I hope your lips grow."

Phoenicia ran, but there was no need because Micky couldn't move. The passengers maintained silence as Micky restarted the car and resumed cruising. Tookie suggested McG's.

On arrival, Tookie and Paunch took their leave without daring to offer condolences to the dead-eyed driver.

At his apartment, Oscar changed out of his work clothes. Given the temperature, he thought it wise to start up his van for the first time in a few days. Once warm, he drove to McG's in hopes of finding the others.

The McG's patrons were packed in three deep at the bar. It was an incongruous mix, the Scummies pressed in belly-to-back behind old alky locals, the latter having laid claim to their stools well before happy hour. Most of the students averted their eyes when Oscar approached due to his association with Micky, but he buttonholed a former classmate, Desmond, who filled him in on the student party roster for the night.

Oscar found Phoenicia and her friend Dolly in one of the booths, each sitting with legs outstretched on their respective benches to ward off intruders. Phoenie drew her stocking feet up at Oscar's appearance.

"Hey, you're Micky's new Scummie boy toy. I guess he thinks he's coming up in the world."

"I dropped out. Where's the King of the Israelites anyway?"

"Fuck cares." She kept her eyes on his. "What a sweet look you got, Scummie toy. Cootchie coo."

Oscar sat and turned to Dolly, who loved to laugh, making small talk easy.

When Oscar rocked back after a bit, he caught Phoenie's icy gray eyes pressing him still. Her toes made their way to his crotch.

Phoenicia had a remarkable face—those cold eyes framed in scimitar brows. She had delicate, cupid lips and a chin dimple like a lewd come-on.

She sat up and nuzzled into Oscar's ear. "Hey, you know, I need some help, baby boy. I've got a problem back at my apartment."

"Yeah? What's that?"

Her tongue darted in. "Problem is, you're not over there doing me right now."

They passed Tookie on their way to Oscar's van.

"Hey man, kegger on Smith, ten o'clock," Oscar said over his shoulder, avoiding Tookie's glare.

Phoenicia had a one-bedroom efficiency in the back of her aunt's house, usually shared with her mom, but her mom, she explained, was "away for at least a few more months, hopefully a lot fucking longer."

"Sweet Aunt Maggie'll stay clear 'cause of the time my guy scared the piss out of her," she said.

"Micky did?"

"Him, nah. Micky's a suck up with old ladies."

The apartment was orderly, with the exception of a cigarette machine Micky had hauled up the narrow stairs and dissected for change. She led Oscar to the couch, shoving over a choir of plush animals, many bearing the scars of her childhood aggression.

On the coffee table, she emptied the contents of two yellow jacket capsules, forming four jagged lines like claw marks. She sucked up three, leaving one for Oscar. Within seconds of snuffing, Oscar was seized with sneezing and awash in tears. Before his vision cleared, Phoenicia was on him.

Oscar bounced like a rag doll, limbs flopping at his sides, but the drug sent Phoenicia's energy level in the opposite direction. She used his neck as a hand-hold as she pumped away, her head high, cursing Micky in ways intended to make Oscar more responsive.

Once Phoenicia tired of the union, she dismounted and left Oscar to give himself up to the barbiturate. She retrieved a baggy from her bedroom and laid out lines of a different granular substance on the coffee table.

Oscar came to around forty-five minutes later in the same position, Phoenicia's face wedged in his armpit. He disentangled her fingers from his hair and rolled her onto her animal buddies.

The mystery drug was still on the table. Oscar did up two lines.

His spine went rigid. He cupped his ears, testing for the origin of the high pitched hum.

When he stood, Phoenicia slid off the couch, joining her pants in a ball on the area rug. Oscar scooped up a half dozen of the Nembutals and walked to the door, turned back, grabbed the baggy of powder, and headed out to his van.

The cold that earlier stung Oscar was now serving as an additional stimulant. He pulled up to the party house on Smith, gnawing new grooves in his teeth.

He caught up to Tookie on the third floor landing.

"Looking just like a soon-to-be-dead fool oughta," Tookie said. "I take it you haven't bumped into Micky yet. You should keep not bumping into him for maybe the rest of your life. Hey, and what's with your zombie fuckin' eyes?"

Oscar held up the baggy. They stuffed a pinch in each nostril.

Tookie looked over the banister. "You didn't bring her, did you?"

"No. She was—"

"Hutt—no, no. Don't wanna know."

"Hey, you know what? Fuck Micky," said Oscar. "What he doesn't know won't kill him."

Tookie pointed out that it was Oscar's life at risk, not Micky's.

The living room, where the keg was stationed, was packed and writhing, the majority of guests being freshman still toe-testing the outer limits of inebriation. Tookie joined the throng, taking advantage of the close quarters to cozy up to a second-year lit major he had been supervising at the dining hall.

Oscar maneuvered through the room like he was trying to match the rhythms of a rubbery Looney Toon, bulging his eyes at the dodgy glances and cackling in response to nothing apparent. He pushed through to the kitchen, which was mostly clear of guests. Lakshmi, the TA, was sitting back a bit from the formica table, the surface of which was slick with splatter from the wash tub-cum-punch bowl.

Oscar was humming something unrelated to the music coming from the living room. He gawked at the ruby-red swill.

"Ummmm. So thirsty. So, so thirsty. Ummm." He brought a cupful to his lips. Lakshmi said something about grain alcohol, which Oscar seemed unable to hear. He used a second cupful to wash down a Nembutal and sat.

Lakshmi had a secondhand book of Escher renderings, littered with clipped addenda and margin note stickies, splayed on her lap. She was outlining a thesis on the works of the graphic designer as part of her applications to the theoretical physics grad programs at Princeton and Cal Tech. Oscar scooted his chair nearer and became engrossed in one of the lithographs, a depiction of monks scaling an endless, unfeasible configuration of stairs.

"You know, Oscar, you were the only one in my class with a feel for the material. Actually, it was clear you already knew it. Why did you drop out?"

Oscar was using a pinky to trace the route of the eternally climbing characters. He raised his eyes. "I don't think it's my thing."

"Bull," she said.

"I'm out of funds. I'm taking the semester off to save up."

"Bull again." She pushed her hair back behind her ears, but the fluffy locks fell back out. "You could easily get aid. Do you want me to help you look into it?"

"I'm pursuing other interests at this time."

"I can see that."

A tall, peculiar, forty-ish looking man appeared. He nodded to Lakshmi in greeting and said hello to Oscar who turned his eyes back to the illustration.

"Lak-sy. Sorry, Lak-a-bie," said Oscar. "Sorry, can't say it. Can I call you Lassie?"

"No."

"Right. Lak-sha-mi, does your thesis propose a formula for how the Penrose triangle will unravel the conunum...conun-der-um of losing quantum coherence when you observe an event?"

She laughed. Oscar looked at her straight-faced.

"They call that triangle an impossible figure for a reason, Oscar."

"Pish posh," said Oscar. "I could formul-tate a...formula."

Ranger pulled up a chair to get a view over Oscar's shoulder.

"Oscar, this is the newly arrived artist-in-residence in the physics department," Lakshmi said.

Oscar spit some drink back into his cup. "Sorry," he said, "I'm sure there's a perfectly asinine expiration—explanation for somebody handing over grant money for that kind of thing. I'm sorry. Did I say, I'm sorry? I'm actually not the least bit fucking sorry."

Ranger smiled. "That's a common reaction, but then that's part of the process."

Oscar laughed. "Ha. I bet that line works for just about any nuisance you come up with—nonsense. What does it that—is it that you do?"

"Do?"

"Paint, sculpt, smudge, urinate? What's the art, artist?"

Ranger sniffed the punch bowl and recoiled. "Yes, all of those, and whatever else it takes to get the concept across. Sometimes not getting the concept across is the objective. Does conceptual art interest you?"

Oscar nodded like a trained horse. "My inner— My interest level is sub-zero. You'd have to do something truthy...uly astounding to get me up to I don't give a shit."

"Ranger's actually kind of a big deal," said Lakshmi. "What was that iceberg piece you did in the New York Harbor? When you almost got the people on that ferry killed?"

Ranger leaned back and crossed his arms. "Gross exaggeration, but I was going for that."

"Dead people?" Oscar dropped his forearms onto the wet table and leaned forward to rest his chin on the surface. His head drifted to the side, eyes back to the Escher drawing.

"No, disruption—plunging people unexpectedly into an otherworldly situation. Those people were never in danger. They were, however, meant to feel threatened."

Lakshmi asked Ranger what drew him to the work at the physics department, but Ranger seemed more interested in Oscar.

"What do you see in that, friend?" he said, pointing to the drawing.

Oscar lifted his head and displayed a confused look, his cheeks drained of color.

"What do you see in that, friend?" Ranger said again.

Oscar's eyes widened. He slapped his hands on the table. He pushed upward to stand, but instead lunged diagonally, upsetting the wash tub.

A red wave broke over Lakshmi. She shot up, sending her chair skidding across the floor. Ranger grabbed the art book as it slid from her lap and held it at arms' length to drain.

Oscar stumbled toward a rear kitchen door that opened on the back stairs.

Lakshmi and Ranger stood listening to the clunks and scrapes as Oscar blundered down the stairwell, and within seconds thereafter to his retching echoing from the alley three flights below.

"Oscar, I need you now."

Oscar fluttered an eyelid.

"You were mesmerized by the Escher drawing. Do you know why?"

Someone outside screamed. "Tell me, fucker!"

Three thuds rattled the van, the third jolting Oscar awake.

"Let's save time," said Ranger, hovering over him. "I'm not a Viking and I'm not a ghost. I'm real and I'm at least partially here and I need answers from you immediately."

"Ooo, hoo, pussy—pushy man," Oscar said. "You don't look— What makes you think you're there?"

"Exactly, this is what I need you to tell me. What is this state I'm in? I feel cold, but there's no pain—no sting."

"Feeling no pain. Me too—neither."

Ranger sighed. "You're there, Oscar, just not fully conscious. But can you tell me what you found inspiring in the Escher drawing? I believe it must have something to do with my predicament."

Oscar tried to turn his head toward the front of the van. "Who put me back here? Am I drying...iving?"

"No, your friend—blond, tall. He always does it—every version. He puts you in the van and drives here. Not too smart leaving you in the cold all evening. But the Escher drawing—I remind you of your fascination only because you won't be alive much longer and I would love to learn something from—"

Oscar lifted a hand to his face and slapped. "Am I touching myself? I can't feel my—"

"This, I know, Oscar: the Escher staircase is built on a Penrose triangle. The path takes three right angle turns and reconnects to itself, so in a sense, it's like a three sided rectangle, which we know is absurd. And yet it somehow registers, optically, as being possible. This would no doubt fascinate you as a physicist. The climbers ascend and loop back around and ascend. Endless nonproductive ascension. They climb and, in so doing, return to the bottom."

"I think I feed— I think I need a doctor."

"There won't be time for a doctor."

"I'm so drunk. Are you the doctor?"

"You took a narcotic as well."

Oscar shook his head. "I had a hickory daiquiri, Doc."

More pounding rocked the van. "Whosit? Damn him. Who's that hitting my van?"

"As I gather, the aggressor outside is insistent that his girlfriend had sex with your blond friend earlier this evening, possibly in this van or possibly at her apartment."

From outside: "Jesus, that's enough, man! What's with you?"

"In other versions, I am exposed to more details," said Ranger, "but it's not easy to, how should I say, cross-check?"

From outside: "Micky, man, cut the shit."

"What is your friend's name?" said Ranger. "The blond friend— looks like you a bit."

Oscar struggled to sit up. "That Tookie? That's Tookie." He struggled to lift his face as though he were trying to break through gauze. He fell back.

"Tookie, ah," said Ranger, "yes, Tookie is being beaten to death."

"No!" Oscar wrenched his head up to his chest. He whimpered and fell back. He tried again.

"Your extremities are not responding, Oscar. Your body is half dead from exposure."

Metal struck metal, like a mechanic pounding out a dent.

"Oscar, the Penrose—"

"Shut. Leave me be, you damn Swede."

"Oscar, why was the Escher drawing meaningful to you? Would you pursue the puzzle of the impossible staircase were you to live on?"

"Live on what?"

"Yes, in other versions, you've already died—many other versions —so chances are you'll soon—"

The other voice from outside: "You're fucked up on Phoenie's powder, you fucker."

Tookie let out a truncated scream.

Oscar's eyes cried out. "On no. Phoenie, she— That's Micky. My fucking legs. Help me up! What's wrong with my legs?"

"It doesn't matter," said Ranger. "You won't need your legs for what comes next."

"Oh my God, just help me get up."

"You needn't concern yourself, Oscar. I don't see this being a version in which you survive. Goodbye."

"Version?"

Ranger, fully naked and semi-opaque, swiveled around in time to catch the opening of the back door and exited, passing through the same space occupied by the killer without drawing his notice. Once a few paces away, Ranger made a motion as if tossing the end of a scarf over his shoulder and climbed the steep sidewalk toward Main.

Micky held a tire iron. Steam rose around him.

"Micky." Oscar coughed. "Micky, I can drive. I'm getting up. I can drive us out of here, Micky."

Oscar turned his head toward the driver's seat. Nothing else moved.

Micky stepped up into the van.

Oscar looked at him. "Phoenie and I, man, don't— Seriously, Micky, I can drive and get us out of here."

Micky let out a wet sob and shook his head. He moaned, his knees sagging. After a breath, he reset his legs and straightened as far as the space allowed. He raised the bar until it clanked against the ceiling and then, wailing, brought it down on Oscar.

CHAPTER THREE

In his confession, the killer describes yet another version of Oscar's death.

Is nothing sacred my mom used to ask all the time. My mom with my old man's cracked glasses at the end of her nose and her red eyebrows up like double questions asking is nothing sacred. Like the world couldn't move forward till she knew. My mom holding up the newspaper at me and saying can you believe these people have no respect for decency and they've got no human kindness and is nothing sacred and asking sincerely. Like a wiseass little jerk like me could enlighten her.

I couldn't help her. She died without an answer. And the pain I feel is because now I could answer. I could answer for all of you reading this and the answer's no. Nothing's sacred so don't waste your life. Don't waste your time believing you have principles that raise you up. Don't waste your time following a code or walking a line or standing up for your friends. Don't waste your breath shouting out reason into that riot of noise out there because it'll get you nothing. It'll get you blow-back is what. Like puking into the wind.

Good intended people trying to guard their loved ones like every principle they believe is another sandbag against the flood well I can tell you it all gets washed out from under you. The sewage rushes in and being right or wrong hasn't got a thing to do with it because good or bad the stinking wash carries away everything you care about.

Sewage is what life treats you like. Nothing is sacred. Nothing.

Which comes to why I'm lying here. What's left of me with one good eye and three good fingers trying as best I can to get this down on paper. I just want to make clear I'm not making things right. If anything it's about making things final. I'm not going to swear to the truth because why would I care about convincing anybody with the weird fascination to read this. You read it if you care to. You believe what you want to believe about me.

I'm beyond deluding myself my words are a warning or comfort to people I loved. The people I spend all my hours trying not to think about. The thoughts away I can't keep away.

Phoenie is here all the time. Phoenie's all mixed up in every sting of pain in me. It's Phoenie giving me unholy shit. It's Phoenie laughing at my sorrow.

And fuck Oscar. Oscar the wasteful empty hearted fuck born one in a million with the mind to really know how the universe works and to even change things like no one's ever known how. He could lift up all the poor lost fools he was that smart but he was too busy pissing all over his life and his brilliant essence has now turned. It's turned now into a poison like acid like benzine blowing acid breaths into me like doing fire breathing mouth to mouth keeping me living. Blowing the horror of life's suffering into me. That's what you are to me now my friend Oscar.

And but there's Mom. When I can still manage to exhale a slow steady breath. When my mind eases I think of my sad Mom because ever since she passed she's been the comforting sorrow in me. She's my cool sorrow. When everything is burning pain then sorrow you know is like the cool pillow you rest your head on.

As for my dad. Will you read this dad and wonder what you did wrong will you be beset with a tenth the pain I'm feeling. No you should go on thinking I'm a delinquent waste. I don't want you thinking of me as a good son gone wrong. Even you don't deserve that but the truth is I'm good. Fuck me I'm good.

I know I'm good because that's the fundamental source of my pain.

Bad would have been easy just like Oscar. Oscar had it easy even dying quick was too damn easy. He hated life in the way only smart people can. He didn't deserve life Oscar. He didn't deserve to die either. He got it too easy both ways.

Life or death nothing comes easy to me. It would have made perfect sense for me to die in that twisted hellfire wreck with Oscar. Only spitefulness could be a reasonable explanation for why I'm alive. Who's spite I don't know. Maybe Phoenie's.

It's for sure not Tookie's spite. Tookie had no spite. By all rights it should be him making me hurt. But Tookie's not the one running this endless torture loop in my head me going like a whacked son of a bitch on him with my whole being in high gear pounding on him and drinking in that hate and still knowing the whole time Tookie couldn't of done shit to deserve that beating. With every swing I'm demonstrating on Tookie what a lying sack of shit he is and at the same time knowing he isn't. He isn't. He wasn't. Sure, he'd lie if he had to Tookie and that night he was lying but it was to save that worthless fuck Oscar.

Lies come in all varieties.

My old man knows a lie for honors sake from a cowardly one and understanding that was a gift he passed on to me.

Even at ten I knew because at ten I remember at the Warren Street Cumbies seeing a puny Puerto Rican kid stuff a damn Popsicle down the front of his jeans. And before I can crack up he's on the run so I trip up the counter guy chasing him down. And do I give a shit about some hairless Puerto Rican kid no but having an ice pop in your crotch is a move worth playing out so I stick my foot out and down goes fat Cumbie counter guy sliding on his fat face into the Little Debbies rack and the kid turns and gives me a grin before hauling ass. I knew then what was coming for me in the world. I knew I'd have mostly nothing of worth but I'd have that understanding of how honor works which just might be worth more.

Tookie same as me.

The Tookie I knew had stones enough on that one night on campus to go for that six-foot wooden cable spool from the maintenance yard. The Scummie boys love these in their dorms for coffee tables he says. We can get twenty bucks for it he says. We're slapping our knees and Paunch is suggesting he give blow jobs to Scummies if he needs the scratch but he trots over and puts his shoulder into that mother spool pivoting it downhill and rolling it out with delicate care onto Wiggins Street. Then we're all up on it beside him helping jockey that mother along Wiggins toward Main and we're thinking piece of cake because the cable is unspooling out as we go and creating just enough drag to keep it rolling at a workable speed.

Then Paunch is saying he wants five bucks out of it and Fleazy says seven and Tookie's telling them to get their own damn spool and as we're carrying on all the sudden no more cable.

I remember thinking in that second that it's not a spool it's three-hundred pounds of trouble waiting to happen. And sure enough it takes off down that hill like a dog slipping his leash a dog tearing off after some bitch.

And I'm smiling now writing this thinking how Tookie must have seen that potential in that spool waiting to happen. Tookie would have.

We all pull up short and watch because no fucking way any of us are catching up to let alone slow that runaway train. Tookie you'd think he'd be freaked but no the bastard is hopping up and down and crying joy like a man sprung from a joyless marriage.

Tookie in that moment he sees how his once promising enterprise which had come to be something damn disastrous just re-became a magical inspiring moment. You recognize right off you don't get many moments like that and Tookie screams Spartacus! I am Spartacus! and oh how Tookie I know wished he could have set that monster ablaze spinning full throttle down into the intersection of Main with the night traffic whizzing by thick in both directions.

I had to half nelson Tookie away from that joyfulness and he fought me because who wouldn't of wanted to see but then he came to reason and goes cutting out of there faster than me cutting between dorm buildings and zig-zagging our way off campus. And then comes the precious sound of those citizens on Main laying on their horns and a good dozen sets of tires screaming out simultaneous. It was just a beautiful moment in time and all sprung out of Tookie's inspiration.

And that was Tookie. I never heard Tookie make an excuse for anything he did right nor wrong. He had the right instincts and he cared for the right things being moments like that. He was as straight-up true to that spirit as any guy you're going to find.

How I'd love that to be my final thought of him.

But Tookie's face the look on Tookie's face when I'm pounding on him that's what I got. Not that he was afraid and not even caring he'd get maimed but just sadness that it was the end of him and me. It's that look that's in my mind like a cigarette burn.

I still hear now as I was hearing then Phoenie going at me with those digs she gets in.

That night earlier in the car she was at it with her digs and all her snickering at me sideways like I'm not worth laughing straight at even as she's stomping off leaving me with it all echoing in my head.

After she slams my car door I'm telling myself no way I'm chasing after her at the same time there's that feeling of relief in getting hurt enough to use. Your brain can almost feel the physical relief of using coming which the self pity and relief cycle is pretty much the worst thing to allow yourself when you're trying to stay clean.

I drop the guys off at McG's and resist going in and so I try back at Phoenie's apartment and then Dolly's then Dolly's sister's to see if Phoenie's gone there which she hadn't so I know she's staying clear of me and conniving something to make me feel small.

And I go to Stan's where I know I'd never see her. It's slow as a Tuesday and quiet which is good. I think I'll cool down and I'll talk to Stan and I'll just drink my damn Mr. Pibb and feel good telling myself if it kills me I'll stay clean just to show her she isn't worth being the cause of me using. Thinking I can manage that makes me feel better.

Gordie comes in who I haven't seen in months and he's fried on crystal all reeky sweat and dry mouth. He looks for me to buy him some shots. There are some words I don't recall and I've got him on the floor with my foot on his throat in order to more precisely share my feelings being do I look like I'm waiting to buy Old Fitz for some lice infested tweeker and Stan put a shot on the bar saying it's on the house just cool it. I toss it back and smash the glass down by Gordie's skull of a face and head over to McG's.

At McG's Tommy K is there drinking boilermakers so I let him set me up and then again. He says he hasn't seen her but thinks he heard Tommy Mullens talking. So I find Tommy Mullens in the corner by the payphone trying to sell dust to some vitamin-deficient Scummler girl. He says no but Tookie was there and I can ask Tookie because he maybe knows. And hanging with Tommy is this wide-ass black guy Desmond I think his name is. He says did I mean that long haired dirt blond guy he was driving a blue van with the Jersey plates and over Desmond's fat shoulder I see that Dolly's scrunched down in the booth but I can see her red frizz poking up. Dolly tells me Phoenie went home by herself which I can tell when Dollie's lying because she's not giggling plus fat Desmond's saying oh yeah that must of been Phoenie who walked out with the dirt blond guy with the blue van with the Jersey plates but that was like a while ago.

I head for the door not knowing where to go next and who do I see ducking me on his way out but Tookie.

Outside Tookie's not stupid enough to be running but he's walking away from me waggling his hand behind saying just fuck off Micky I haven't seen her she's probably passed out somewhere.

I picture her in bed just after she's been with you and her face all rosy and that upways curl of her lip and her fingers still around you from when she was guiding you and I'm caught up to Tookie and get a good shove in from behind just when he's at the van sending him in nose first.

Phoenie put out for you Tookie I ask him. Bet you knew she'd put out for you tonight. And he's all, What the fuck What the fuck. And I whack him in the ear like a damn ten year old because you don't do that to Tookie and him not come back swinging at you which would get things going real good. But no he's still all leave me alone I didn't touch her. Leave me alone.

I keep at it but can't get him to hit back but I sure enough can drag him by the hair around to the back of the van where I know Oscar has his tire iron jammed behind the spare. I want to see what scaring him shitless will do is all. And I can sure enough whack the van by Tookie's head for emphasis. And I'm jabbing him in the ribs with it and keeping on him. I'm thinking about her and Oscar. I'm thinking what damn sense it makes it was Oscar screwing Phoenie and how much pleasure she's getting from me knowing that and how much harder she's coming just knowing I'd know that.

I'm punching it up into his gut and I'm whipping back and slamming it on the van by his ear and seeing Phoenie swallowing him and where she always puts her fingers and her throat groan and all the rest she does and I'm not whacking the van any more.

I'm not hitting metal.

Tookie is down.

Tookie is lying there. I don't know how long it took me standing there but I see what I've done. I know what I've done.

Everything around me and in me gets this horrible way about it. I want to puke it all out of me this horrible horrible feeling. And in the middle of that wretchedness something so insane happens like an unholy vision I'm not meant to understand it's this huge white guy he steps down out of the van naked as fuck. He's so big and white as a ghost I can't think I can't breath him just walking away. The way he walked I can't explain. It was like he didn't need the ground like he pretended to walk just for show. And then he checks back at me like he knew all about what was happening. He knew what I did and but he's not worried or even that interested just a look back at me for my benefit to let me know I don't know what.

I hear the tire iron clanging on the ground. The cold whiteness coming off that guy as he walks up to Main as insane as it was I want to hold onto it to try to understand but I can't.

I'd done enough bad shit to know what was coming. The thoughts start to come. I'm asking myself how can I fucking die before I feel the gut sickness. And I'm crouching there by Tookie and the thoughts start coming and pain I can't shake it out of my head and I try to scream it out of my head.

I'm on my knees and I see the keys in Tookie's hand he had them the whole time. Fucking hell. His palm is laying open right there in front of me the red marks fading from the keys he held onto so tight and it's like he's offering me the keys there on his open palm.

I hug him and I pick him up still so warm across my back and there's the blood in streaks and puddling up around the street ice already turning frothy with freezing at the edges all along the van and my footprints dragging it back and forth.

The pain and sickness and the thoughts are so awful I can't possibly scream them away and at some point I'm there in the van wheel in my hands and if I calm at all and find any clearness it's just in knowing there's no chance for me. Maybe others learn to live with that pain. Maybe they never feel it. I know I always will. But I know what I can do is start up the van and drive. Just go hard and fast enough to turn off the wretchedness and turn off the yearning for hope and love that's at the root of my pain.

Just drive to the end of your life and close your eyes.

CHAPTER FOUR

Having survived his accident, Oscar recounts the process by which he brought an impossible figure into existence.

The more science I learn, the less sure I am of anything.

Science is built on theories. Theories are supported by suppositions. Suppositions are uncertainties. Scientists prove nothing in the absolute.

Any scientist worth anything knows there's a great chance someone will soon come along to prove his theory wrong. In fact, the vast majority of theories throughout history have been proven wrong.

And so it stands to reason that all answers to all questions are equivocal. Everything is ambiguous. Anyone intelligent enough to understand this principle who gives you a firm answer is lying, and of course anyone not smart enough to understand is usually not even close to giving you information of value, which means pretty much all information that comes your way is bullshit.

The futility of it all can be depressing. Then again, this great fallacy is terrific news for dumb, wishy-washy people who give vague answers because, although they're no more right than smart people, they're no more wrong most of the time.

Lakshmi is the smartest person I know but, like most truly smart people, she burns too much brain fuel defending theories that will scatter like coke off a mirror when the next fool sneezes. I do like her, even though she puts on airs like she's certain about things when certainty is a pipe dream. On occasion, though, she reveals that she's got the kind of fundamental doubts that I admire in a person. If her belief system has been sufficiently undermined, I might see in her the same kind of futile yearning that I'm subject to, yearning for unattainable proof of something—proof of anything. It makes her desirable to me. I'm not saying it's a sexual attraction, but it's as good as one. And hell, if it is, so be it.

So getting Lakshmi to reveal that part of herself is a favored pursuit of mine. I've learned that the surest approach is to wear her down with talk, which I can sometimes manage when I'm in a chatty mood, either via substances or due to lack of sleep or hours at a formula or some combination thereof. Once her dialectical fiber is worn threadbare, she'll squint in a headachy sort of way. At those times I am convinced she is having those doubts and despite herself is saying with that nuanced expression, Oscar, I think you're an arrogant shit, but I so want you to take me to bed.

Absurd, I know, but again, it's probably not a sexual thing.

That night in the dining hall, Lakshmi and I were twenty minutes deep into our conversation but she was still shy of the squint-point. I'd been in my room at work on my formula for going on three days, interrupted only by my four-hour dinner shifts, one of which I'd just completed, powered on five cups of gray dining hall coffee and a healthy pinch of phenylpropanolamine derived from some diet pills I'd filched from a sophomore girl's dorm room.

"OK, sure, the Escher drawing triggered my thinking on the formula," I told her, "but it was only a trigger. He was just an artist. It's not like he was capable of anything beyond optical tricks. I'm not stealing from Escher. Newton didn't steal from the apple tree."

"I didn't say you were stealing," she said.

"You implied it by not fawning over my brilliance."

"And by brilliance, you're referring to these delusions of grandeur you're experiencing, imagining you can build a physical model of something that doesn't even make sense in two dimensions?"

"Grandeur—sure, in lieu of identification, let's call the hallucinogen coating my sinuses that night Grandeur."

She worked at freeing her desert dish from the plastic wrap. "Are you going to show me your proof, genius?"

"Not ready yet. Maybe tomorrow. Or it could take another year, or most of my life. But maybe tomorrow."

"And with this schedule, you want me to recommend you for a grant? Have you met the department chairs?"

"The comb-over dudes, yeah—pale, sour smelling."

"That's them, and I believe only one is formula-literate, so you'll have to do your pitch in English."

"I've been practicing in the mirror."

"Oh? Let's hear it." She laid her fork down and leaned back.

"Right. I'll say to them— Shit, I just had it."

"Seriously, you better—"

"No, wait—the stone towers. I'll say, picture yourself standing on a tall stone tower. You're looking out across rapids—a churning river—to an identical tower, and someone appears, or maybe that someone was there first, it's not clear. And it takes some time to realize that the other person looks like you, and maybe exactly like you, but with the distance it's hard to say. You think about waving but you don't. And you ask yourself if the other person is thinking about waving too.

"It's a warm, bright day with a nice breeze and you feel like you could stand there for hours just watching the river plunge by and spray off the boulders and carry by felled trees and old tires and busted roadway signs. You think, maybe I've already been here for hours."

Lakshmi made a "move on" twirl with her fingers.

"Right, you circle around the parapet to the other side. Further away in the opposite direction is another river and, beyond that, another stone tower and another figure, very possibly a replica of you as well. You spend some time there watching. You see the figure circle around to look at, presumably, someone on another more distant tower. When you circle back, you see that the nearer person is absent, and then he returns from, no doubt, gazing out in the opposite direction.

"You wonder at the pattern of rotations around the towers, not just your movements, but all the movements of all your doubles. And soon your thoughts are more consumed with the patterns than the river or of the other towers or the other figures. And at some point when all thoughts of all the gazers are consumed with patterns, something happens: The thoughts align in just the right way, the result of which is that all but one tower disappears. And later on you find yourself again on a tower wondering if you've been there long, and the process repeats itself."

Lakshmi sat forward and poked at her lemon meringue square.

"I'll tell them it's my allegory to explain quantum phenomenology," I said. "They'll nod. They'll smile knowingly and say yes, yes, beautifully put. But of course it won't be because the concept is un-puttable. The allegory is utter bullshit."

She pushed her tray to the side. "They're not stupid."

"They're moderately stupid, certainly way too stupid to take on this science. I could tell them that, but this way they'll think I think they're smart enough to understand, and at the same time they won't want to challenge my theory for fear of revealing how little they understand, and that reluctance to question me will be a cornerstone in the foundation of our relationship as granters and grantee. It'll be a fine outcome."

"It's not utter bullshit."

"Well yeah, I mean—"

"Your allegory. It could be a useful allegory."

"Only useful in illustrating the futility in using words to explain the science. The science can only be expressed in the formula, and then only symbolically. No other language is up to the task. And so if the comb-overs aren't formula-literate, they're too stupid to understand."

"Please stop calling them stupid."

"I'm not being judgmental. I've got nothing against stupid people. My family are stupid people. So are all my friends, except you."

"I'm pretty sure I'm not your friend."

"Why not?"

"Because you're a total shit. Do you ever think of taking me to bed?"

She didn't say that last part, but she was doing the squint thing. What she did say was, "Because your friendships don't end well. You haven't talked about Trudy at all, by the way."

"Tookie. When did I ever talk to you about Tookie?" I said.

"Never. Sorry. I'm sorry about Tookie."

"Tookie was among the least stupid of my friends."

"Sorry. Yes. I'm sorry."

"What about my friend Micky? Are you sorry about Micky?"

"No. Do you want me to be?"

"No. Fuck him."

A week and a day and a few hours later, I was at McG's taking a health break when Large Swede showed up. He convinced the unibrowed Bruins fan next to me to give up his stool, which was a relief, until Swede started talking.

"Can I buy you another of those?" he said.

I polished off my glass. "I don't think I'm your type. And no, anyway, I should get back to my whiteboard." I stood.

"You don't remember me, Oscar?" He turned his head to give me mug shot angles.

Yes, he was familiar in a dream-reality sort of way. Up close and actual, he for certain registered as odd enough to be hallucinatory. His face was washed out and elongated, like I was seeing him through distorted glass. He had shaved the lower two-thirds of his scalp all around, creating a platinum blond, medieval bowl cut. His sideburns swept in a scythe arc from his earlobes down to his jawline and up to connect to a repugnant patch, like a Hitler mustache misplaced on his lower lip. It was a disturbing use of hair, and yet I was most unsettled by his scarf, which was wound and knotted with enough complexity to frustrate a good man of Gloucester.

"My name is Ranger," he said.

"Right, I've seen you around the department, you and your scarf."

"We met at the keg party the night of your accident." He snapped his fingers to get the bartender's attention.

I sat back down. "Do more of that, man. I love what Franky does to people who snap their fingers at him."

His eyes brightened. He snapped his fingers again.

"Ranger, like hangar? Why do you pronounce your name wrong?"

"I assumed the name as part of an art project." He took a pencil from his pocket—one of those orange, waxy ones with the peel-string. He wrote his name on a beer coaster—®Anger.

I put the coaster in my jacket pocket. "Thanks. If you're for real, this might pay off my student debt some day. You trademarked anger? You don't seem like you do anger well enough to lay claim to it."

"No? What do I seem like?"

"Like the pretentious, self-aggrandizing sort who would change his name under the pretext of art."

"Do you remember me from the party?" He grabbed another coaster, signed his name again and put it in his pocket.

"No sir, I have no memory of that night, sir." This was not true, but the memories I had made so little sense, I found amnesia to be the wisest position to take with the police and campus administration, and I saw no reason to open up to a nosy, self-obsessed Norsemen.

Franky laid two glasses of draft on the bar without asking for our order—not unusual, but instead of his standard punishment for the finger-snapping, he gave the Swede a pickled egg.

"I'm an arts fellow in your department." He shook the saucer and watched the egg wobble. "This is what the bartender does to people?"

"No. I don't know why he gave you that."

Ranger smiled. "People treat me differently, sometimes well, sometimes not, but always differently. Do you remember me from the party?"

"You're a repetitious son of a bitch, aren't you?"

"Do you remember me from the party?"

"No, did I talk to you?"

"Yes."

"Did I marvel at the idiocy of an arts fellow in the physics department? Because if I didn't, I'm not sure if I can live with myself."

"Rest assured you did."

"What kind of art do you do?"

"The kind that defines what art is."

"You do realize that's circular logic."

"Perhaps."

"Wait, were you in my van that night?" I wasn't sure why I asked that.

He paused like he was making an effort to remember. "No, I was not in your van."

Again, I felt a pang of familiarity from that pale, vacant, floating face. "Because if you did happen to be in or in the vicinity of my van that night," I said, "I have Lieutenant Meyer's card. She'd be real anxious to talk to you."

He popped the egg in his mouth and passed it down with a few chomps. He took a cautious sip of beer. "What more do the police need? I understand they have the killer. And they have your testimony, do they not?"

"I gave no testimony because, as I said, I have no recollection. All I know is I woke up on the pavement with a lot of red and blue party lights swirling and the smell of burning Micky-flesh."

"Do you doubt that Micky Green killed your friend?"

Franky, rinsing glasses behind Ranger, heard that. He watched for my response.

I leaned in. "Micky's prints imply he did the deed, but my prints are on the murder weapon too. And Micky's face has the same kind of gouge mark as Tookie, so not everything makes sense."

"It was your tire iron? Are you a suspect as well?"

"Not that they're saying. Who told you it was a tire iron?"

"You did."

"Nope."

He took another tiny sip of his beer, eyes still on me. "So, for the sake of expediency, the police are hoping Micky Green starts talking, assuming he doesn't succumb to his burns."

"Right, assuming he wakes up. If I were him, I wouldn't."

He watched me drain my glass.

"What's the punishment?" he said.

"There's no death penalty in Mass, unfortunately, so I guess Micky's sentence would be, remain conscious for the rest of your life."

"No." He flicked his head in Franky's direction.

"Oh. Your beer would have mistakenly made its way onto your lap, assuming it could get past your fucking scarf."

He smiled. "How's your grant writing going?"

"For what?"

"Lakshmi didn't say it was a secret endeavor. Should I whisper?"

I felt betrayed, but then realized Lakshmi had succumbed to whatever was loosening my tongue. "It's going nowhere. I imagine you hire some fancy-pants grant writer. I don't have those kinds of resources."

"I do, but you don't need a grant writer. I can fund you, or at least I can devote part of my grant funds to your research." He took another fake sip.

"You're full of surprises, Gunnar. Why would you do that?"

"I want to see your idea realized, just like you do. And I'll want the rights to be the first one to try it out."

"Wow. You've got no goddamn idea what you're asking for, and I doubt your grant has a spare three-hundred gees to dispense with."

"You don't need that much."

"For starters, I need computerized fabrication equipment capable of taking CAD/CAM formula instructions. Only two companies in the world make it."

"My art fabricator has all that. He can turn out anything you give him in a variety of materials."

"You have an art fabricator?"

"Yes, how do you think I produced my Thousand Polanski Dicks series last year—perfect 3D replicas in granite with—"

"Please. So you're not shitting me? You can fund me?"

"Yes, I can and will."

"Still, you have no idea what you're getting into."

"There you have it. That's the concept of my piece."

I didn't know how to respond. What came out was, "Are you going to drink that beer for real?"

He threw his head back and faked a laugh loud enough to hush the bar. Once he had everyone's attention, he angled back on his stool, lifted his glass above his head, and poured the contents into his lap.

Ranger went dark for two weeks. I was resigned to having been handily screwed with when one drizzly morning he rematerialized outside the dining hall. I was late for my lunch shift.

"Go on in and give them your resignation." He was leaning against his classic Mercedes drinking tea out of a Thermos that looked as old as the car. "I'll take you over to your workspace. You can get started."

We drove to a middle school on the north fringe of town, one of those flat-roofed, flesh-colored joys built in the '60s. The grounds were in respectable shape, but a good many windows were filled with plywood. Someone had spray painted DRINK THE RICHES BLOOD [sic] across one.

All the doors were padlocked. Ranger had the key to an entrance around the side by the loading dock.

Once inside, he excused himself to find the circuit breaker. The fluorescents crackled on along our hall and the one that intersected it.

The place was in shambles—books stacked and tossed against

lockers and furniture piled in some areas like someone was planning a series of bonfires. We passed an intact display case. A lone trophy bowl had been left containing what appeared to be human stool.

"The school is in limbo," Ranger said. "The board is weighing sale or renovation. I paid them for use of a classroom and amenities for four months. Will that be long enough for you?"

"What amenities? How much did you pay them? Do I get a stipend?"

"You won't need any money. You'll get everything necessary to do your work. Will that be long enough?"

"No way of knowing."

"Will that be long enough?"

"Yes. Is there food?"

He turned and continued on. "We'll have your meals delivered. The girls' showers are serviceable. You'll want to avoid the boys locker room."

"Nothing new there."

We made a left turn and entered a double-size chemistry classroom, pungent with Pinesol. One row of lab tables had been pushed to the side to make space for a single bed, wardrobe cabinet and minifridge. The walls accommodated sixty linear feet of chalkboards.

"You sure know how to romance a girl, Olaf. Do we have tunes?"

Later that afternoon, he led in an audio tech who pushed before him a library cart stacked with gear.

"Tell Julian what music you like," Ranger said.

Julian had a fuzzy goatee long enough to obscure the slogan on his t-shirt and Gene Wilder hair.

"Nothing with words," I told him. "Anything repetitious and featureless and free of associations, preferably atonal."

"Atonal like Schoenberg and Berg, or like La Monte Young and Cage?"

"The Bergs. Reich's percussive stuff will do. Maybe Riley."

"Riley can be quite lyrical."

"Yeah," I said. "Fuck Riley. Cecil Taylor."

Julian nodded.

I copied my formula to four chalkboards. By the second evening, I was working them in tandem, pitting variations against one another.

I removed the wall clock, but kept the shades up on the windows. As the hours past, the light drifted through the room and Julian's music droned, humming like blood in my ears. When stuck I often found myself daydreaming my way along the periodic table mounted high on the wall, a yellowed relic, printed when the world was ignorant of seaborgium, bohrium and meitnerium.

I got a few hours rest each night and got back to it each day at sunrise. Delivery guys came each day at ten, two and eight and laid out meals that I often noticed hours later. Ranger entered in silence daily around noon and headed straight for his seat at the teacher's desk, re-stationed in the back corner. He spent his days scribbling notes, sketching what looked like the same half-abstract figure in endless variations, crossing and uncrossing his legs, sometimes draping his gangly arm over the desk in a grotesque sideways writing posture. On occasion, he stood for a Zen saunter along the blackboards, tracing my figures in the air with his hand-shaved pencil. Once daily, he documented the formulas with his Hasselblad, noting each film frame, time and date in his sketchbook.

I slept in random patches around the clock. Ranger stayed through many nights, often still awake with me when the morning sun cut through the side windows.

"I can't tell if you're the most patient son of a bitch alive or the most monotonous, Gunnar," I said one morning. "Why are you here? Go somewhere. I'll send up a smoke signal when I'm done."

"No, I need to be present each day. It's the function I've assigned myself during this stage in the process."

I remember only a few more involved conversations with Ranger, the first maybe a week into "the process" after I wiped a large section of the formula from one of the boards. I backed away to stare at the void left by the eraser.

He stepped around me and squinted, as if waiting for messages to reemerge through the cloudy swirls.

He turned to me. "Why did you do that?"

"What?"

"Remove that. Did you have a setback?"

"No. I'm advancing the formula to the next phase."

"What phase did you just complete?"

"Establishing a pattern. I like to apply the principle to different dynamics and see if it works—if the pattern holds."

"Did it?"

"No, not in that variation."

"Did you have a setback?"

"No, like I said, I've learned what makes it fail and I'm moving on."

"That's not what you said."

"OK. Nevertheless."

"What's the next phase?"

I'd gone nearly thirty-eight hours without solid sleep. I backed into a chair, settling harder than I'd intended and sliding back a foot along the mottled linoleum. "You know what, Ranger? I'm not interested in explaining it to you."

"What's the next phase?"

"You can hear me, right?"

"Yes. What's the next phase?"

"Christ. I think of the next phase as bend it 'til it breaks. You put stress on the principle. The breaking point tells you something. It's like crashing a prototype car to see how to improve the design."

"What are you expecting it to tell you?"

I let my head fall back and closed my eyes. "This has become physically painful. Look, you know that cartoon guy? Maybe it was Wile E. Coyote. Yeah, you know when Wile E. Coyote puts on Acme wings and jumps off a cliff? Somehow, through the delusional exuberance of necessity, he flies, and it all goes great until he thinks, fuck, coyotes can't fly."

"No. What happened?"

"He plunges to the bottom of the canyon."

"Why did he want to fly?"

"Not relevant. The point is, explaining how I think really messes me up. It makes me think I can't think. Plus, you're so far from being able to understand the science, it's not funny."

He nodded. "Think of a way to explain it to me." I heard him walk back to his seat.

"I thought you said not understanding was key to your process."

"That was in the initial phase. I'm moving my process forward."

I initiated another conversation a few days later, mainly because thinking about how thinking about how explaining it might fuck me up was fucking me up. I downed my third cup of coffee and called him to the board.

I drew a square. I drew a second, overlapping the first, the same size, displaced by half the height of the figure and half the width. Then I connected the like vertices with diagonal lines.

"A Necker cube," he said.

"Ha. Imagine that. They teach geometry in Sweden, do they?"

He narrowed his eyes. "I'm actually from a country called Canada. You may have heard of it."

"Sorry, no."

He nodded toward the board. "Why did you draw this?"

"So yes, Ranger, as you may know, the Necker cube is a textbook example of an impossible figure. I've drawn it here, of course, in two dimensions but it registers in your mind as a three dimensional object because brains tend to do that shit involuntarily. Your brain, for whatever sublunary Darwinian reasons, tries to convince you you're seeing things in 3D. Your brain recognizes these chalk lines as a cube, but because of the way it's drawn, is unsure which sides are foreground and which are background. The figure teases your perception. Your mind oscillates back and forth between the two possibilities in a futile attempt to reconcile which is in front. At a point, your higher reasoning kicks in, assuming you have some, and you write it off as an optical trick. You with me?"

"Yes. The impossible figure, in other words, exists only in that it is as a deceitful collusion between your conscious perception and the physical world."

"Damn, that's good. Write that in your little sketchy-book. OK, you're ready for lesson two: the ramifications of quantum mechanics and the observer effect."

He folded his arms and leaned his butt against the chalk tray.

"Right." I went on. "Well, as quantum theory goes, reality is in a state of flux until observed. A material occurrence carries with it the potential to take on any number of physical states. But it's only the act of watching that particular something occur that sets one of those states into permanence—that phenomenon is known as the observer effect. The act of observation limits all the possibilities down to a single one. And said observation prevents the possibility that any of the other states will occur."

He nodded.

"Great. Now for the big 'but.' We ask ourselves, what happens when we observe, not your average, run-of-the-mill occurrence, but an impossible object? Your brain says, 'Is this side of the box farther away from me or closer?' You look at an Escher drawing. 'Are those stairs ascending or descending?' Your mind is trained to set one of the object's states into permanence but, failing to reconcile the two possibilities, is unable to and so the oscillation continues—back and forth. When presented with an impossible figure, it's as if your mind perceives two states at once."

"The mind refuses to make a choice and set one of the states into permanence," he said.

"Bingo." I tapped on the board. "These are just chalk lines—a 2D representation of an impossible 3D object. But suppose we could construct the impossible object in three dimensions—a sculpture, in art-talk—a real, live physical manifestation? The object could—"

I watched Ranger cock his head to the side and realized I wasn't talking anymore. I hadn't planned to get this far in my explanation. I needed more words.

"Go on," he said.

"What I mean to say is, if we can build it in three dimensions, we might create—and here's where words are vague approximations—a time-slash-place where all the object-slash-event's possibilities can be experienced simultaneously."

Ranger straightened his back against the board. He smiled a little. "One would experience a number of versions of the event. How many?"

"Hard to say. With a point-zero-three margin of error, somewhere between a dozen and one hundred and forty-four thousand, I think. Anyway, that's the theory of what would happen were we to construct a 3D Necker cube."

"I will experience an untold number of versions of the same event."

"That's the theory, although how a human brain would process all the versions is a ridiculous thing to try to project, almost as ridiculous as putting a human into that kind of danger. And you are human, despite appearances, correct?"

"It will be an historically significant artistic achievement. I'm not concerned about subjecting myself to some danger."

"You got the historic part right. We're not talking about possible paper cuts here, Lars. This is danger of the historically unfathomable kind. I warned you about that from the get-go, but now maybe you understand how crazy it would be to—"

"Will I remember all the event versions later?" He was looking at me, but not really. And he was blinking, something I'd never noticed him do before.

"I'm not sure there would be a later for you, Ranger of Canada."

He froze for a moment, then he nodded.

He nodded for some time.

"Now, assuming there is a later," I said, "you may remember all the event versions in series, although they in fact happened all at once, if once would be at all meaningful as a word, or you might remember them in a different random sequence every time you think back on what happened, that is if happen would still be the applicable verb. Or if situations would still exist. It's tough having to use words for shit like this."

He tugged at his stupid little soul patch and flapped his lower lip.

"Would it really be happening," he said. "Would all of the different versions of the same event really happen, or would my mind just think they were happening?"

"Well, there's that verb problem. If a real occurrence is defined as one that is set in permanence through observation, then multiple versions of an event observed simultaneously should in theory all be happening. But tree-falling-in-the-forest-wise, if you can't document what happened or tell us what happened afterwards, did anything happen? Not as far as the world and your legacy is concerned. Will we ever know what you experienced? Can't say."

Ranger returned to his desk and sat. He stared at the formula for a few minutes. After a time, he lifted his Thermos cup toward his lips and saw that it was empty. He put it back down.

I went back to the board and erased the impossible figure drawing. I wrote in its place, "IF IT CAN'T BE DOCUMENTED IS IT ART?"

"You leave that to me," he said.

"What?"

"Documentation. Monet looked at the same haystack at different times of day under different light and painted all the versions. Most people marvel at the variations in palette he used. For me, it wasn't about color. It was about time. Was there ever a more glorious way to document time? Don't worry, I'll find a way to make a record of the things I see and hear and feel. All my art training has prepared me for this."

"You won't have anything with you. Extraneous objects will add too many variables. No camera. No sketchy pad. No notebook. No recorder. No clothes."

He tapped his temple.

"Well," I said, "as long as there is a way for you to relate everything afterward—but your observations will not be accepted as evidence because your mind and the event are, as you say, in collusion. There will be no a priori data, only what you've observed and what your mind is telling you happened."

"You've just described my art. The subjective observation and the art will be one and the same. If I prove your theory in the process, that will be part and parcel of the art. You see how important that distinction is? I'm not creating art with science. I'm creating science as a byproduct of art."

I laughed. "Call the process whatever you want and make whatever claims you want. It's my formula and my rocket launch and you'll be the chimp in the capsule."

"I will be like Leonardo, who brought art and science into glorious conspiracy."

"Leonardo is a great name for a chimp."

It was hard to conceive of Ranger having friends. He clearly took no enjoyment from sharing time with people, not in a human-to-human sense. His interpersonal skills were solely geared to getting his way, typically by exploiting people's compulsions. He knew setting me up at the school was like supplying a junky. He knew I couldn't resist the draw of the formula any more than he could resist the opportunity to do momentous art.

The school had no working phones, no mail delivery, no radios or TVs, which was perfect for the first couple of months. The lack of distraction was bliss.

About ten weeks in, though, I began to lose focus. Solitude began to hang on me like loneliness, despite Ranger's omnipresence. At difficult turns when I should have been self-correcting and bearing down harder, my brain sought diversions. Lakshmi was in my head, luring me off course. At first she voiced my doubts, and that could be helpful. "What the hell did you do that for?" Fine. But then she began to play the tease. Not good.

I was also occupied by thoughts of my father back in Newark more than was healthy. We'd last talked on the phone shortly after the van accident.

"I can get a train up there and then take a bus out to your hospital from Boston," he'd said. "But they say you're OK, but I can if you want."

"That's OK, Pop. You'll miss too much work."

"Marv can put on another damn driver for a couple days. Bastard owns me—owes me." He'd been drinking. I could hear Charlie Parker rolling out notes behind him. Dad would pour his first rye rocks and put late era Coltrane on the turntable. By the third refill, he'd have worked his way back in time through Monk and Mingus to Dizzy and Bird.

"No, forget it, Pop."

I heard him suck on his Parliament. "They say you're a lucky son of a bitch, Oscar Boy. You feel fortunate to've gone through what you did?"

"I think you've got that twisted up. What they mean is fortunate to come out the other side alive, Pop. There's nothing fortunate in losing my van and my friends."

He hacked. "To hell with alive. Alive is nothing. Every fool is alive. You went through something damn profound. And it wouldn't have been profound if it hadn't've nearly killed you. Not many people get a chance to get nearly killed, percentage wise, and when they do, they squander the opportunity to learn from it. What did you learn, Oscar?"

"This is about Mom, right? Are you saying you learned something because you made it to shore and Mom didn't?"

Another drag and a slow exhale. "Maybe, Oscar. Maybe I lost that privilege because I couldn't look at it for what it was. Maybe you've got more guts than me and maybe you're smarter than me. Hell, you're a damn sight smarter than me. Maybe you'll see it for what it is."

"There's nothing to see, Pop, beyond the foolish shit my friends and I did. My shit was the most foolish, Tookie's the least. So, consequently, Tookie, who was the least responsible for what went down, is the most dead. Micky is only responsible for reacting like a creature of his kind is apt to react. Now he's worse than dead. I'm the guiltiest of them, and I'll stroll out of my hospital room free as you please next week."

"If you don't learn a lesson from this, you'll be the most dead of them, Oscar."

"Is that what you really want for me, Pop? To resolve this for myself? I get the sense you'd be more satisfied if I went all dead inside like you. I hate to disappoint you. I'm fine."

"What's that supposed to mean? I don't want you dead inside. I want you to find some peace is all."

"Not a problem, Pop. I'm on it. Really. Goodnight."

One night, I found myself talking to Ranger hours after he had gone for the day. I dug out my stash for the first time since the accident. I considered the dexies and then a pretty little square of windowpane acid I'd been saving, but deferred to better judgment. I pulled out two buds and returned the collection to the safety of my boot. As I rummaged through the classroom lab drawers for something I could fashion into a pipe, Lakshmi wandered in, as if summoned by my deviant behavior.

"He called you, didn't he?" I said.

"Who?" Her eyes went right to the board.

"The Iceman. He calleth? He's been pacing more than usual. Today, when he screwed up a drawing, he tore it up into ragged strips instead equilateral segments, as is his usual practice."

No response. She backed up to lean against one of the lab tables, scanning the formula laid out on the chalkboard. She was wearing her brother's formless high school soccer hoodie, her hair half-captured in a rubber band.

"You look nice," I said.

She flashed me a dissuasive look.

"I really need to see people more often," I said. "People are nice. I wish Ranger was a person."

She circled her finger in the air around a section of my proof. "This here is wrong."

I joined her at her gazing post. "It used to be wrong, historically speaking," I said. "Actually, yes, it's still wrong until you get here. It makes this happen." I pointed to a portion eight lines down. "So it's retroactively correct."

"But that can't really happen," nodding at the latter section. "It's—"

"Impossible—or at least it is now, but won't be if I can work it out."

Her jaw sagged. She pushed off from the desk and stepped closer to the board. She put her middle finger in her left ear and began tracing the spiral out to the edge, then back inside, eyes running through the formula, back and forth. I recognized the condition and stepped out to smoke.

When I returned, I found her still finger-in-ear. She was bent forward at the waist and rocking from her knees, as if in mourning. I sat at Ranger's desk, taking advantage of his absence to deface a few of his peculiar figurative drawings.

I was involved in embellishing one with mustard from the previous day's lunch parcel when I heard the tapping of chalk. Lakshmi was inserting a line.

I waited for her to finish and joined her at the board. I erased a portion of her revision and replaced it with a third the number of characters.

She grunted and considered, then added another expression a few lines down.

We went on that way for a while, a couple of hours I think. At some point as she bent down to work on a lower portion, I slid my hand under her sweatshirt and traced the protruding nubs of her spine. She pushed me away with her left hand as she wrote on with the right.

When exhausted, she sat in a student desk and put her head on her forearms. Her eyes were still on the formula the last I recall before I nodded off on my bed.

I woke when the classroom door closed behind her. I saw that she had altered the last two of her additions.

Ranger arrived on schedule.

"Did you two get intimate?" he said as he tore the disfigured figures from his sketchpad and began cutting them into equilateral segments.

"Yes." I went to the board and continued.

For the next week, I made decent progress, lost again in the work.

One night, as Ranger sat at his desk, I stood in position a few paces back from the board, reviewing my formula and as usual when in that posture and so immersed, I felt content—or more accurately, I thought I felt what I feel like when I think of myself as feeling content.

Then, like that coyote flapping his arms over the canyon, all in a moment I lost the illusion. I became conscious of stuff my body was doing, disturbing stuff, like the condition of the inside of my cheeks, chewed sore, and my left leg, jittering at insect frequency, and the vinegar odor rising from my pits, and the ache in my upper back from jamming my hands deep into my pockets. The thoughts set off an icy pang in my gut and a swarm of prickles up the back of my scalp, and I saw the linoleum beneath me swell and rise.

I shuffled past Ranger, down the hall and out into the night in nothing but my shorts. I broke into what I imagined was a jog, but was likely a panicked scramble to a gas station about a mile east. I used the pay phone to call a cab.

The driver refused my IOU for Percocets as payment so, when we arrived, I asked him to wait in the driveway.

I ran around to the staircase behind the house, up a flight and knocked. I could hear movement inside. I pounded louder.

Phoenicia yanked her door open.

"Phoenie, lend me a five-spot for the cab, will you? We'll talk. I want to talk, you know, about things."

She shivered as if resisting a great urge. I saw her right hand was hidden behind her hip just as she sprung with the icepick.

She spiked it into the fleshiest part of my right deltoid. I went stiff, hung up in her bat shit eyes. She gave the handle a further shove until the point resurfaced out the back.

I remember hearing a squeal that must have been me. I fell back, freeing myself from the pick and blundering down the stairs.

Phoenie stood above panting, her sweater off one shoulder. She looked around, as if acknowledging the pleasant evening. Then she tossed the icepick behind her into the living room and pushed by me.

"I can't do you here," she said over her shoulder. "We'll take the cab to your place."

I awoke to throbbing in my shoulder and slow, raspy breathing. I peaked over at Phoenie and remembered. Then the bed rocked again and I saw Ranger, towering overhead. He had his pointy Italian boot on the cot frame, jogging us at two-second intervals. Phoenie slept on. She was on her back beside me and across me, splayed naked.

"You don't want to wake her up by doing that," I said. "It's not safe."

I stood and adjusted the clotted ace bandage that had crumpled up into my armpit. The bed linens were streaked with blood.

Ranger picked the top sheet off the floor. He snapped it out into the air and let it drift down over Phoenie, face included. "Please ask your guest to leave."

He left for an hour, returning with a Thermos of coffee. Phoenie was in the shower. I was trying to ease on a t-shirt.

He studied my movements. "Have you been shot?"

"No. Icepick."

He nodded. "I believe I explained that having people here could compromise the project."

I took the coffee from him. "I don't recall you saying that."

"Having people here could compromise the project."

"It won't happen again."

"You're lying to me."

"Most likely, but I think I can get back to work now."

Ranger fetched his camera and documented the bloodied sheets before taking his usual position at his desk.

I moped down the hall barefoot and into the moist warmth of the locker room. I caught her emerging flushed and gleaming from the shower area, smelling great from the same discount shampoo I'd been using for weeks. The cold lights behind her set the steam aglow and softened her.

I sometimes see a young women for a passing second on the street, maybe stepping off a bus, washed in the sunlight bouncing off a shop window, somehow deemed virtuous by the aura. I see unaffected goodness in her bearing and in her simple gestures a purity of intent that makes it impossible to imagine her being bitter or spiteful. And I imagine being with her in a house somewhere, comfort without challenges, someone who will at most be annoyed with all the selfish shit I pull, and maybe in her worst moment leave for her sister's for a puff of weed and a glass of Riesling. She'll return with takeout. I'll love her.

At that moment, the light should by any right have treated Phoenie with equal grace, but even in her defenseless nudity she came off as menacing.

I sat on a bench. "Is she the one?" I realized I'd said it out loud.

"What?" she said, sniffing at a used towel she'd pulled from the pile beside me.

"You haven't said how you like my place, Phoenie."

She dropped her head to the side and rubbed at the fall of hair with the towel, her breasts shimmying. "This here, what you got going, is no doubt some wicked weird shit, and you're much more of a faggot freak than I thought. What are you doing in a freaking school?"

"You can't tell anybody about me being here."

She smiled in her crooked way. "You're building a bomb."

"What? No, hell no."

"Tell me what it is and I won't tell anybody."

"Seriously, I can't. Just be a friend."

"Ain't your friend. I'm the girl you fucked when you wanted to act criminal. I bet Micky'd be real interested to know what you're doing here." She ran the towel over her tummy, between her legs, and down to her ankles.

"Micky's unconscious, Phoenie. You might find piquing his interest a challenge."

"I'm going over to see him. You should come."

"I don't think my lawyer would understand."

"Suit yourself. If he's awake, he'll be real interested to hear what's going on here."

"You're way off base. It's not even something Micky would get upset over—were Micky conscious."

"Might be authorities hanging out their'd be interested."

"Why are you screwing with me, Phoenie? You think I'm to blame for what Micky did? He tried to kill me. Does the guilt get flipped back to me because he's lying there burnt to a crisp?"

Her eyes welled up. She pulled her sweater on and picked her panties off the bench, but sat with them in her hands. "You're a shit stain, Oscar. I'm suffering in pain. I got pain you don't know. Everybody's suffering in pain but you."

"Oh, I think I've suffered—am suffering."

She snickered. I realized I was holding my shoulder.

She finished dressing, then headed for the hallway. "You coming or not?" she said.

They had put Micky at the end of the corridor and left a couple of rooms vacant between him and the other patients. Phoenie smiled as we approached the uniformed cop sitting outside room 528.

She did a little chassé and pointed at his face. "Hey, you're Jack Morgan's kid?" He had buzzed red hair and a mustache that might have made a sixteen-year-old Irish brat feel grown up.

"That's right. Brian."

"Brian, damn. Your old man used to hang out with my Uncle Tommy? Tommy Logan."

"Probably." He moved his eyes off her chest to check me out. "I didn't know Tommy Logan. Heard good things, though. And I was told you'd probably come by and I was told you're OK but not anybody else outside of family and especially not your friend here."

"What? Oscar's OK," she said. "You're sitting right here. What's he going to do?"

He looked at me again. "You can't go in the room."

She stepped forward and took hold of the doorknob. "Come on. Let him. You can put him in cuffs if you want."

"The hell he can," I said.

Phoenie laughed and turned the knob.

"He woke up," said Officer Brian.

The room was dim, just the monitors casting blue shadows. Phoenie walked around the bed, slowing as she checked out the manacle on Micky's ankle.

Micky rolled his head over so he could see her with his right eye, the only part of him exposed. Everything else was mummied or hidden by the tented bedsheets. He sucked in a snorkel breath and barked a shallow cough.

I felt the top of my head taking on weight and my vision went woolly around the sides. I leaned against the wall beside Officer Brian. Then the odor from the room hit me—piss, sour meat, and menthol, and something like alcohol, but much stronger. My legs felt useless. I let myself slide to the floor.

Officer Brian looked down at me and sniffed.

"He's my friend, you know," I said. I put my chin between my knees.

"I can't discuss the case," he said.

"You don't know what happened. He could be the real victim for all you guys know."

"Can't discuss."

"Great. Another repetitious son-of-a-bitch." I grabbed the back of his chair and got back on my feet. "What's with everybody? Did they raise the price of words?"

"Watch your lip." He looked at his watch, then down the vacant hallway. "Look," he said to me, "you got three minutes in there. Put your hands in your back pockets.

It took a second to register. I complied.

"Keep 'em in there. If I see so much as a knuckle I'm going to break it and run you out."

I entered.

"And don't discuss the case," he called.

Phoenie was still on the far side of the bed, chin down. She shook her head. "I came to see you, baby." She reached for his arm but crumpled her fingers mid-way.

He coughed hard. For a long moment, he went silent. Then he sucked in another gargly breath. "So?"

She waited for more. "So what?"

Another breath. "So, what do you see?" he said with a dry lisp.

She was shaking. She opened her mouth, closed it, and hunched her shoulders away from us.

"Hey, man." I approached the bed. "How are the pharmaceuticals?"

He swiveled his head my way. The eye was red where it should have been white, but it was Micky's eye and still said everything about him.

He stared, like he was trying to work something out. He mouthed something.

"Sorry, man. I can't—"

He cleared his throat. "Stoned as a gnome."

He kept me pinned with the eye. "So either you're alive or I'm..."

His throat went thick with phlegm. He closed his eye while he worked to clear it.

He resumed. "Either you're alive or we're both dead."

"I'm alive. You're alive. You don't believe in the afterlife anyway."

"Then why? Why're you alive?"

"Luck. Stupidity. I don't know. I can only remember some shit that I can't make sense out of. Nobody knows the truth about what happened. What can I say, I—"

"OK, stop."

He took a moment, then went on. "Stop that fucking nonsense. I know what I need..."

I waited while he gathered strength. "I know what I need to tell you," he said, "and then you need to get the fuck out. I love you, but you need to get away from me."

"OK."

"I've gotta tell you a thinking...a thing. Fuck, I can't think."

"What, man?"

"It's about the truth. I need you to know because you'll be there instead of me."

"Where?"

"Here. You'll live. I'm fucked."

"OK."

"The thing about the truth is, you can't tell the truth because there is no truth."

"OK."

"There's no truth because nothing is sacred."

He went quiet. Then, after a while, he asked if I understood.

"Yes. Nothing is sacred, so there is no truth."

He closed his eye and let his face fall away from me.

Phoenie went mum on the way back. I offered to feed her and get her drunk but she shook her head and watched the city bleakness slip past her window.

As she stepped out of the car, she croaked something under her breath.

I leaned over into the passenger's seat. "What? Hey, do you want me to come by maybe tomorrow? Are you OK?"

She looked back and repeated herself through her teeth. "I may not be able to not fucking kill you if I see you again."

I sat alone in her driveway for a while and tried to devise a way to distract myself for the night since I had absconded with Ranger's car, but all thoughts led back to Micky's mono-stare and "sacred truth" (i.e., lack thereof) and his cavernous breaths and morgue smell. I headed back to the school and my stash.

Knowing that Ranger would be waiting in the classroom with his agenda of a face, I lit up a soft, deliciously blond, morphine-veined hash nugget in the hallway, planning to offer it to him upon entry, something guaranteed to piss him off and maybe disorient him long enough to distract him from whatever he was undoubtedly going to piss me off about, but what I saw flipped me into the disorientee position.

Ranger had cleared the furniture to the sides of the classroom to make room for his work. He was crouched, butt naked, arranging long strips of reflective mylar into the shape of an impossible chair, about eight feet square. It was a straight-backed design that I recognized from his sketchbook. The legs were situated so you couldn't tell which were in the foreground or back, a pretty astute extrapolation of the Necker Cube. Laying it out in mylar was crafty too because the rippling, mirrored surfaces pulled in the surroundings and made you want to step into the thing, like Alice's looking glass.

At that moment, his lungs inflated with hash vapor, nervous system abuzz with the promise of a lovely initial rush, the reflectivity of Ranger's figure took on a tantalizing meaningfulness. And as the silver-cold hash ticklies flushed from my cheeks up into my ears, the undulating mylar surface, at once both an object and a representation of everything in the room that light could bring to that object, all made manifest by me, the conscious being doing the observing, as if given an endless landscape and an observer of endless vision the object could at once absorb and reflect all of creation, sparked in me the realization that I too, as part of the immediate environment, was both a passenger and pilot, an observer and creator and participant in the object's bottomless macrocosm.

And then, like I'd simply licked my finger and flipped to the next chapter, a new extension of my formula incorporating my just-then-conceived New Theory of Reflectivity made itself known to me.

I exhaled.

I smiled at Ranger. I felt compelled to express my admiration. "I get it. It's a chair."

He turned and sat on the floor, throwing his stork legs wide, his balls spreading out on the linoleum. "Yes, it occurred to me that we may not know how long the performance will take so I thought I may as well sit comfortably."

I giggled, I think. Yes, I must have giggled. "That's not a comfy chair. Maybe add puffy armrests? An ottoman?"

"It cannot have style. It has to be devoid of style. Minimalist."

"Right."

I took another hit. Some time passed. I said, "Minimalism is a style, you realize."

He stared for a second, looked up at the formulas on the board and then back at me. "Minimal is more sciency."

"Ah. Well OK."

He looked down and reoriented his penis so he was symmetrical.

"By the way," I said, "it's not a performance, it's an experiment. And the possibility that you would be able to sit on an impossible object is non-existent, unless you have an impossibly shaped ass. I'm no expert on guys' asses, but I'd say yours is fairly conventional. I'm thinking there's a better chance you can crawl inside an impossible cube, or at least your chances would be infinitesimally shy of impossible."

He put his arms out behind him and leaned back.

"And you're naked why?" I said.

"It's part of my process. We'll need your fabrication schematic soon. I told Luis to expect it next week."

I coughed up hash phlegm. "Whoa, I haven't started modeling. I don't even have a 3D workstation."

"Your computer will be here tomorrow. They loaded the applications today and installed the extra RAM you wanted."

It was my turn to stare. "And you know what? Your mylar gave me a fresh idea, so I'll need more time to work that out and—"

"I told Luis to expect your schematic next week," he said.

I relit the pipe and sucked the remainder of the lump down to gray dust. I closed my eyes and pictured the formula, new amendments snapping into place with a wondrous certainty that almost made me want to believe in purposefulness, knowing of course that such foolishness would pass out of me soon after the magical blond hash mist, which I released from my lungs at what felt like the pace of a morning glory collapsing with the waning of the light.

But it was probably not all that slow.

"OK, sure," I said when my lungs allowed me. "I can render a model. I can do that."

He nodded, pulled in his legs, spun on his ass, and began rearranging his figure into a conventional Necker cube.

During the next few days, I roughed in the formula revisions and settled down at the workstation to undertake the CAD/CAM modeling, step one of which was to confirm that, by all established scientific dogma, it was impossible to translate an impossible object into three dimensions. Step two was to do it anyway.

It was the final hurdle, a challenge I dreaded and itched for. I'd hoped that, once underway, a path would reveal itself, but instead I succumbed to overthinking. Absorbed as I was, hope/dread-wise, Ranger's impending deadline slipped my mind until he reminded me one afternoon that he'd summoned Luis the Fabricator for the following day.

Once Ranger left for the night, I had the presence of mind to call out for three pizzas, six liters of high-caffeine soda, and two fifths of vodka. I accepted the delivery and barred the classroom door with two filing cabinets and a lab table.

Some time before noon the next day, the door handle rattled. Another hour passed and another rattle, accompanied by anxious conversation in the hallway. The chatter went on for some time, rising steadily, punctuated with less and less polite handle jiggling. By and by, all went quiet.

A few hours later, Lakshmi appeared outside, pressed between the bare forsythia bushes and my windows. She motioned at the sky or, more specifically, the rain ripping down from the sky. When I turned back to my workstation, she tip-tapped on the glass with a coin. It was just the right level of annoying and went on until I got up. I pulled the window open.

"Tell Pope Ranger that the ceiling needs another coat of paint," I told her. "He should get the reference."

She dropped a heavy tote bag through the opening before grabbing my shirt for leverage. Once inside, she shook her head to whip the rain from her hair and removed her wet sweatshirt.

I returned to my work. After a few minutes, she pulled a chair up and watched. She smelled like damp cardboard undercut with cloves.

I sat back and looked at her. The limp condition of her hair was an improvement on its usual fluffiness and, lacking the volume, allowed her eyes to take command. Lakshmi's eyes were about as steady and dark as eyes get on people.

She retrieved a wide coffee table book from her bag. It was titled, "The Treachery of Images."

The cover showed a public plaza. Crowds had gathered around various photos, displayed in rows, each broader and taller than the viewers. I could make out images of common objects—a plumber's wrench, a bicycle pump, a floor lamp. Lakshmi flipped the book open to a shot of the artist, taken at the exhibition. The composition was symmetrical. On the left was a life size, full figure image of Ranger against a white background. On the right was the real Ranger posed and dressed identically. Both held placards reading "I am I".

She closed the book. "Ranger is apparently the real deal," she said. "Have you read about him?"

"No. Real what? It looks like he's trying his best to prove that he's real. Is that what you mean?"

"He's obsessed with illusion and reality and the false distinctions between the two. But more relevant to your current situation, given his standing, he's got the art world dangling for his next project and big money people to answer to if it flops."

"I want to say, 'Well, that's his problem.' Hell, why not? That's his problem."

She nodded, her eyes drawn to the splayed takeout boxes and crust shards littering my work table. "Well anyway, I've known this about him for some time, and so I expected him to come up with some sort of public performance somehow dramatizing your theory but, stupid me—" She smirked. "When he came to fetch me today and introduced me to whatshisname—"

"Luis."

"Yes, Luis. When he introduced me to Luis, I realized Ranger is looking for a real world application of your theory." She tittered.

And then she laughed, grabbing my bicep, leaning in over my lap. The book slipped and fell, edge first, onto my instep. I screamed, but she held fast to me, shaking in hysterics.

"That was the basis of our agreement, yes," I said, once she had collected herself.

"Oh God." She sniffed and dabbed her eyes with her sleeve. "But that can't happen."

I led her to the board and showed her the changes I'd made. I showed her Ranger's reflective cube adorning one of the walls and then the formula amendments again. She pointed out a flaw, which after less than an hour, we corrected. And then she stiff-armed me back to give herself some thinking room and started that ear thing that she does.

I rinsed out two plastic cups and cracked open the vodka.

We sat and talked theory most of the night. She was unrelenting, prodding around every crevice of the formula for more fault lines. She failed to find any. In fact, in defending the work, I clarified some points for myself.

"Damn, I think I know what the CAD rendering needs."

"Well that's perfect," she said.

She drank an impressive amount, nearly keeping pace with me, and at a point we pulled up chairs for our feet and stretched out, side by side. We talked on.

After some time, her head slipped over onto my shoulder. "Would you be more comfortable on the bed?" I said.

"Yes, I would, if you weren't here." She sat up in her chair. "I understand in the abstract what could happen. I just can't visualize it. Can you? Do you know what it will be like?"

I was toasted. "Oh, you're talking about the experiment."

She smacked my bad shoulder.

She tossed her empty cup back over her head and stood, wavered and steadied herself against a desk. "Jesus, what's going to happen to Ranger? I mean really—what's going to happen to him? You can't let him do it."

I flopped onto the cot and braced for spins. "You know what, Lashy— Hey, are you sure I can't call you Lassie?"

"Very."

"You know what? There is absolutely no way to visualize, let alone describe in language that people use, what'll happen to our intrepid Ranger. Ranger's a flying starling out for a little…flight. He's a starling about to get sucked into a jet ocean…engine. Try asking a starling if he'll come out the other side. Ask'm if he'll still be a starling when he gets there. Ask the fucking starling if he'll split into little starling bits or if he'll split into a whole fucking flock of identical starlings, each present in alternate realities with different possible outcomes in a—"

"OK, stop, you've broken the allegory."

I closed my eyes. "Jet ocean. Funny."

The next morning, Ranger beat on the door nonstop until I answered. His inability to mask his revulsion at the state of the classroom inspired me to bow deeply and waltz my way back to the cot where Lakshmi lay, fully clothed. Ranger picked up stray items on his way to his desk.

A bit later, when I flip-flopped past him in my flip-flops on my way back from the heads, I noticed the large manila envelope centered on the desk in front of him.

"Sinister," I said. "It must be for me."

"Yes, we'll need to go through it this morning."

Lakshmi was still in bed, arms crossed over her eyes.

"You want some diner hangover food?" I called to her.

She nodded, then groaned at what the movement did to her head.

"Take us out to the Gold Star for breakfast," I said to Ranger. "You can bring whatever that is."

There's something about a mouthful of runny, over-salted eggs drenched in Tabasco sauce that makes everything tolerable, at least in that moment.

"OK," I said, "now."

Ranger put down his spoon. He laid the release form on the formica and showed me where to sign, then returned to his oatmeal.

It was easy to see the passages within the boilerplate paragraphs that his lawyer had customized.

"So you accept the possibility that you may be killed," I said. "But you don't acknowledge that being killed could be one of the better outcomes. Maybe this part here should also say, 'I absolve Oscar of any and all horrid consequences beyond all imagining.'"

He held up a hand. "Don't. I need to go in uninformed."

Lakshmi paused her coffee mug on the way to her lips. "But Oscar is informing you. He's telling you it's too dangerous."

"Maybe uninformed is the wrong word. I'm saying the artist must be seen facing the unknown."

Lakshmi and I traded looks.

"Is it?" he said as he chewed.

"What?" I said.

"Unknown, or do you have a good idea what will happen?"

"I have numerous theories and they all have a common motif which is that anything could fucking happen. You've heard the axiom that anything that can happen will happen given enough time?"

"Yes."

"Well, we're producing a circumstance in which that truism holds even after you've removed time because we may be making all possibilities of what can happen all happen in a given moment."

He nodded, eyes in his mush.

Lakshmi huffed. "Can you just explain why you feel compelled to do this?"

We waited for him to scrape up the last glob. He pushed the bowl aside and looked at her.

"It will be great art. It should be, by what I can see, the greatest of what art can be."

"It will likely be a godawful disaster," said Lakshmi. "Why will it be art?"

"Because I'm an artist and it will be my experience."

She put her mug down harder than intended and then pulled a wad of napkins from the dispenser to clean the slop-over.

"Will this make me an artist too?" I said.

"No."

"Good."

"If it's art then, I mean—" Lakshmi rubbed between her eyes. "I don't understand the meaning of the art."

He sat back and pivoted to get room enough to cross his legs under the booth table. "The meaning is in the act of an artist experiencing something that no human has experienced. The meaning is in me wanting to create the greatest work of art of all time—in me being absolutely committed to that objective."

"And you're willing to give your life for this? For fame?" she said.

"No, you misunderstand. The fame is a bi-product of the art, not the objective." He looked out the window to the damp boulevard. "I've committed myself to art my entire life—body, soul, and mind. This is the greatest act I could ever hope to achieve as an artist. There's no particular need to live on once it's accomplished."

I laughed. "Living typically comes with its own inherent need to, you know, survive."

"But you would like to live on, right?" said Lakshmi.

"Of course, yes. But it doesn't matter that I would like to live on. That desire, as Oscar might say, needs to be eliminated from the equation."

"I wouldn't say that. You're thinking of the Professor from Gilligan's Island."

Lakshmi's mouth was open. She looked at me and shook her head, just a little.

Ranger was looking at me too. He patted the agreement.

I picked up the pen and signed.

Luis, as it turned out, was not the accommodating sort. After the barred door incident, he stomped back to his workshop in Queens and rejected all of Ranger's entreaties to return. He said he'd taken another project and "fuck you you think I coming all the way back up that shit hole excuse of his town to beg audience with your brat sorompo," as per Ranger.

About ten days later, I handed Ranger a disk. "This is the CAD file. Did you get Luis to sign the thingy?"

Ranger nodded. "The NDA. Yes, before he came up."

"Then send him this. Either he'll grasp it or he won't. If he can't see what this means, he's no good to us anyway."

Ranger sent it by overnight courier. For four days, he tried raising Luis on the phone, but no answer.

The delay suited me fine. I was counting on a healthy setback of perhaps a month or two so I could refine the formula and fabrication schematics and possibly build in a failsafe mechanism to keep the bottom from falling out of the fabric of reality and such.

Ranger, meanwhile, descended into a funk. The signs were everywhere. He put down his sketchpad one afternoon at less than a right angle relative to his row of fine-tipped pens. That evening, he allowed food-soiled paper plates to remain in the wastebasket for over an hour before bagging up the trash. By the third day, he'd stopped shaving. The pencil thin lines of his stupid side-burn extensions began to blur.

On day five, it occurred to me that I might be deprived of my comfy gig were Ranger to lose heart. I turned to my stash for a solution.

Ranger was at his desk, crumpled forward. I clicked my tongue.

"Do you know what these are?" I held the baggy by the top two corners and danced it like a marionette.

Ranger lifted his chin from his forearm. "They appear to be dried mushrooms."

"Correct. More specifically, mushrooms of the magical persuasion. Part of the magic is their tendency to taste worse than the manure they're grown in. How about this?" I revealed a jar of Nutella from behind my back.

"That's Nutella."

"Two for two. I bet you're feeling better about yourself already. This one's on me." I lifted the third item onto the desk. "Wonder Bread."

I used a box cutter to do a fine mince on the mushrooms, stirred them into the Nutella, and made us each a globby sandwich. Ranger wolfed his down without initiating a gag response, something I'd never myself managed.

I turned off the overhead fluorescents and lit a bunch of Bunsen burners. The room was all blue and flickery, even before everything took on the visual equivalent of an electric hum.

Ranger was silent. I asked if he was going to puke. He shook his head. But he didn't look like he was getting off on the right foot. Ranger was exhibiting symptoms of distress—peripheral eye darts, a pincer grip on his earlobe, tiny bird warbles.

(Note: Mushroom experiences are calmer than acid trips and they don't go bad too often, but they can surely go bad, which is why it's critically important to remember all Six S's of a Great Trip: finding the proper setting, assuring a calm situation, planning for an adequate session length—I don't remember a couple—and sharing the undertaking with a sitter, meaning an experienced guide.)

I told him "easy," drawing out the first syllable like a mantra. He watched me and followed along, rocking forward and back with each repetition. I nodded encouraging nods.

Ranger brightened. He stood and dashed from the room. I sprang to my feet in pursuit, wished I hadn't, and puked into the nearest desk drawer.

I was gargling with orange Fanta when he returned, carrying a piano stool. He sat near the center of the room and closed his eyes for about five seconds—although, it's hard to be precise since time was curling into the dippy stage. Then he opened them wide enough to a tad freaky. He closed them again. To that sequence, he added a partial rotation of his stool, about fifteen degrees at a time, so that with each move he'd reopen his eyes on a new aspect of the room. This he repeated for what felt like a long time.

I was mesmerized by his fastidiousness, even though a mildew stain would have kept me entertained at that point. "What are you seeing, Stretch?" I said.

He dismissed me with an inadvertent finger-flutter that proved fascinating enough to earn a place in his routine. He continued on, rotating and fluttering.

I suggested he rotate in the opposite direction. He said, "Why?" and I said, "You realize you're on a piano stool," and he said, "Yes," and I said, "You get shorter when you rotate counter-clockwise."

And thus the laughing commenced.

There's nothing like laughing on mushrooms. It's laughter that's far greater than yourself. It's as if the inanity of the cosmos takes gaseous form and blows through you. The entire neighborhood convulsed with our gusts of laughter.

Of course, you can't laugh all night, but the aftermath is almost as gratifying. The effort leaves you relaxed and receptive and— I'm going to use the word smushy here.

Ranger and I bonded like—well, like two slices of Wonder Bread glued together with psilocybin-laced Nutella. It wasn't hard. In fact, it's pretty hard not to find common ground on mushrooms. The mind naturally seeks out affinities, all of which seem incalculable in their significance.

I pulled my mattress onto the floor and sat with my back to the wall. Ranger grabbed his sketching supplies and joined me. He crossed his legs and raised a pencil.

"Is there anything that feels as comfortable as a pencil in your hand?" He sketched female forms in the air.

I thought deeply. "A fork."

"Yes. With one you devise, with the other you devour."

"Dichotomous."

"Perfection."

We talked about body surfing, ejaculation, tail feathers, the Alamo, Davy Crocket, Veronica Lake, Credence Clearwater Revival's Lookin' Out My Back Door, pin wheels, the skid mark patterns on squash court walls, iron filings, the magnetic North Pole, Veronica Lake (again), walking, the word "phonetic", frozen grapes, and glass. We talked about glass for a long while.

It took me I'm-not-at-all-sure-how-long to realize that we had stopped talking. I'd pulled a thread from the bottom of my t-shirt. I managed to tie it to a lock of my bang hair and was blowing it out from my face, watching how the squiggles played against the blue Bunsen emanations. I glanced over to see that Ranger had drawn a tobacco pipe on his sketchpad, one of those pudgy, curvy Sherlock Holmes types.

He saw how it captured my attention. "You know the Magritte painting of the pipe?"

"Nope."

"Underneath, Magritte wrote, 'Ceci n'est pas une pipe.'"

"Damn. No shit. Damn."

"It's called The Treachery of Images."

Ranger inscribed "This is not a pipe" under his drawing.

"OK," I said.

"So what goes through your mind?" he said.

"It's not a pipe. It's a drawing of a pipe."

"Go on."

I thought a bit. "And in the same way, if an actual pipe were in your hand, you would only be seeing light reflecting off of something. You're not really seeing the quote-unquote real pipe either."

"Go on."

"And so Marguerite is saying many things that we see are not what we think we're seeing."

"Magritte. Is that it?"

"Yes, I think so."

"You didn't take it to its conclusion."

I thought again. "Nothing is what it's supposed to be. Absolutely nothing."

He smiled. "Magritte's painting may be the greatest work of art ever produced because it explains in indisputable fashion the nature of reality, or I should say, the fallacy of reality. You see, while science has yet to determine what reality is and isn't, art has already proven with a simple image and a few words that reality is a fallacy."

He was wrong, but I agreed without question.

"And Magritte's painting will pale in comparison to my new work," he said. "And the fact that I don't understand the science is not at all important."

"Our new work," I said without thinking.

He stared at me for what seemed like a long time. "Our work."

The mushrooms were a success. Ranger enjoyed a post-trip halo that sent his despondency packing. What I hadn't expected were my own aftereffects. I never wanted to like Ranger. We were now tripping buddies. The universe won't stand for someone deriding his tripping buddy. And so, the worst part of it was, I was no longer at all sure I didn't give a shit if he died, and I was pretty sure the experiment would kill him. Had things followed their course, I might have found myself in my own muddy funk the next day, but as luck would have it, we were awakened by Luis pounding on the exterior school door.

Outside, Luis's crew of three—Ty, Amber, and Parker—sat on the tail of the panel truck, legs swinging in near unison, waiting for the go signal to unload. They looked alert and underfed, and at the same time committed and jaded, like graduate students. Luis, on the other hand, could have been the foreman on a moving crew. He was road-worn, meaty, round shouldered, and tattooed, right up across his shaven scalp.

As I approached, he gave the crew a nod. Amber hopped to the pavement and slid the ramp out while the other two unbelted the load.

"Wow, you've got a lot of shit," I said watching the first of many carts roll past packed with scaffolding sections, machine parts, test scopes, power supplies, wiring, tarps, and tools. "Did you bring your whole shop, just in case?"

I said this because, while I had supplied Luis with a CAD plan for the impossible object, I'd provided only vague suggestions as to how one might build or carve or mold something that can't exist.

Luis's arms were crossed high on his substantial chest. "Tell me, what I do for a living, Esé?" Nothing in his look read as sarcasm.

"You're a fabricator?"

"And you think our artist friend inside he know how to fabricate? You think any these artist genius they know shit about how to bring about a creation into this great wide world?"

"I take it no is the response you're looking for."

"How 'bout you? You know how to fabricate this thing you want?"

"In an abstract sense, sure.

"That what you want, an abstract sense?"

"No?"

"You lucky to have me, el cerebro. You work with me before, you would have think, well Luis, he come with exactly what he need for this job. You are Frank Lloyd Wright and if you says to me, build my mile-high skyscraper, I come knowing. I figure out how to pour the foundation. I figure out how flexible the walls. The material, Esé, is all about material and how to make that material give birth to your vision. You have a vision, young Oscar?"

"I do."

Amber took a cart over a sidewalk seam too hard and a lighting stand clattered to the pavement. She looked at Luis while she stooped to retrieve it. He raised an eyebrow.

"I have to warn you, though, Luis," I said, "that my vision is rather disturbing. And no disrespect, but do you understand what the hell you're getting into here?"

"You mean this quantum mechanics theory you imagine up?"

"Yes, that."

"Well, first, the theorem you write is a beautiful thing. I marvel at such beauty and right away I know this will be Ranger's greatest work. So my choice it was made. You see, friend, I have two advance degrees in mathematics and engineering. I know what to look for in beauty. I study at Instituto Tecnologico do Buenos Aires. You hear of it?"

"Nope."

"Exactly. Is best in all Latin America, but I come here with my degrees and I apply for jobs and apply and apply no one give one skinny turd about what I know. And so I'm working in a machine shop and some artist woman, she asks can I help her build a vagina house that will float on the East River, and of course I did no problem and that was how I get started. So yes, Ranger know I am the one to make this real and you will soon as well."

We stood for a while, and then I said. "I ask this not to question your qualifications, Luis, but because you seem like a sincere hearted hombre. If you know your shit, and I sense you do, this could get pretty messed up. It could fuck up your life, is what I'm saying."

He laughed, baring what seemed like too many white teeth. "Oh yes, fucked up most for sure." He leaned close and put a hand on my shoulder. "But artists, you know, they have much to teach us scientists. And in one thing, I have learned especially with Ranger. If there is a chance to make great art, we must. It is in the soul of all great men. It is critical. Are you a great man, Oscar?"

"No?"

He turned back and pointed out the sidewalk seam to Ty as he approached with another cart.

"It is critical," he said again.

Luis marched down the corridor, arms swinging, stepped into the classroom, grunted at the condition of things, turned, continued down the hall, ducking into doorways, and finally staked claim to the gym for the staging of the event. He ordered Ranger to lease out the cafeteria kitchen as well. "I must treat my people with proper food. Very critical, food. You and your boy genius, your eating is crime."

Ranger headed off to the school board offices to negotiate an extension to the agreement.

Luis's people swept and mopped the gym floor. They rolled out paper pathways and pushed in their carts. Ty and Amber organized the gear along the room's periphery while Parker checked off the inventory list. Then they set to work assembling scaffolding, proceeding methodically under such shorthand directions from Luis as "up, up, four more, up" and "angle less—no, no, angle less, other way less."

The master fabricator kept his workers locked in his sights nonstop, insisting they triple check every connection and, even during breaks, quizzing them on next steps.

I saw him break focus that first day for only a few minutes, when Lakshmi appeared late in the afternoon. He reintroduced himself with a queasy joke about passing her off as Guatemalan when bringing her home to Mamita. Lakshmi did an unconvincing job of disguising how charmed she was by the attention. Luis carried on with his supervision, but flashed his pearlies her way at regular intervals.

By that first evening, the crew had a substantial framework in place, a rough cube about twenty feet high, wide, and deep. Luis applauded to signal an end to the day just as Ty was preparing to set up the first of the laser devices. Luis showed me one of the mounts. "Adjustable in three dimensions to within microns of prescribed positions," he quoted from the manual.

Early the next morning, Luis called us to the cafeteria where he'd whipped up a breakfast substantial enough for Che's guerrillas. He slid trays out onto the serving line—fluffy eggs, frijoles bathing in peppery black juices, steaming tortillas, shredded chicken, crispy fried plantains, and salsas spanning the spectrum from lime green to blood red. The crew dug in without comment.

Lakshmi arrived, shuffling in like she was wearing her bedroom slippers. "Oh my God, look at the food."

"Before dawn?" I said.

She scratched her belly. "Luis invited me over. Hey, why do you look so shitty?"

"Thanks. You should see Ranger. Luis has him so on edge, his turds are coming out sideways."

"But no, I mean what's with your—" She didn't normally look at me for any length of time.

"Did you cut your hair?"

"Wow. My hair was long—very long. You're not sure? You care about me that little?"

"I've never cared about your hair, if that's what you mean, not until now. You look like a gulag escapee. Why did you do it?"

"Oh, I don't know—despondency?"

"Over what?"

"Let me think. Oh right, something about Luis figuring out how to test a hypothesis that should for the sake of humanity stay strictly hypothetical. Something about maybe tearing a run in the stocking of reality. Something about Ranger's impending death, if he's lucky."

She forced her eyes away from my scalp. "Don't be dramatic. And don't be self-pitying. I hate that."

"I'm not sure you're allowed to hate someone you don't care enough about to note their hair length."

"Why are you taking this Luis seriously?"

"His laser array makes sense, which I find frighteningly impressive—frightening because if he has the brains to take it that far, maybe he's got it all worked out."

She shook her head. "Very slim chance."

"Slim odds of bringing on the end of the world is not comforting."

"We'll just have to talk to Luis and see what he's got." She turned for the food line. "And I don't hate you, exactly. That characterization lacks nuance."

After the meal, Ty and Parker cleared the plates while Amber performed the elaborate ritual of banding her unwieldy Afro. I pulled my chair next to Lakshmi who was allowing Luis to show off his schematics.

Lakshmi was pointing to a set of rectangular icons labeled "QCL".

"Quantum cascade lasers array," Luis said. "They do extreme rapid switchy-switch, back-forth."

"Between what?" said Lakshmi.

He shrugged, like it was obvious. "States, grounded and excited."

She looked at me.

"Physical states of matter," I said.

Lakshmi rolled her eyes. "Yeah, I know, but I'm just kind of—I mean, those lasers must be so expensive. You can't have this many."

"Two-hundred and fifty-six we have spaced along all vertices." He patted the rendering of the cube-shaped frame structure. "They are on loan—Ranger's foundation, it found us a source—but yes, crazy expensive, very excellent gear."

I could see that Lakshmi was getting the same sinking feeling that hit me when I realized Luis had a grasp on laser technology far beyond his station.

"They will draw," he said, "the Necker cube."

Lakshmi was starting to rub her eyebrows. "So, wait, the lasers describe the Necker cube figure, and they switch at tremendously rapid speeds between the adverse and inverse states, and what—?"

Luis was clearly enjoying the moment.

"Basically," I said for him, "the objective is to fashion in physical form what your eyes are tricked into seeing when you look at an impossible object on paper. It'll go from an optical trick to— I was going to say 'to reality' but I think I'd need to come up with a new definition of reality to make that claim."

"You're trying to tell me that when you look at a Necker cube and it plays that trick on your brain so you think it's flipping between foreground and background—that illusion—you're saying that thing will actually be happening? Physically? No, that's ridiculous. Yes, they're damn fancy lasers, but we're still talking about a figure drawn with light, not matter."

"Hey, I'm just the theoretical physicist around here. Making it real is Luis's gig."

Luis was grinning. He wrapped an arm around Lakshmi's shoulders. "You see, cariño, but you don't see. Look, here." He pointed to some spiral-shaped squiggles on the diagram. "These are nozzles. They apply the virtual substrate."

"What virtual substrate?" I said. (Sinking feeling again.)

Lakshmi joined me in interrogating Luis. We took turns filling in phrases for him when his communication skills fell short.

In a nutshell, Luis had adopted a process similar to one they use to manufacture delicate electronic parts—a precise method that adheres super thin film to substrate forms, like microchip patterns to silicon wafers. But his bat shit-brilliant twist on it was to have the light emissions from the lasers serve as the substrate instead of solid matter.

"The nozzles," Luis told us, "they spray the—What you call it, the gaseous form aluminum?"

"Evaporated aluminum," said Lakshmi.

"Aluminum vapor," I said.

"Yes, yes. And it, the vapor, it passes into the laser, the beam."

"Into the laser's path," said Lakshmi, "and then, oh, wait, wait, it—"

"Acts on the vapor—" I said.

"You got, yes, it— What is called, makes itself solid again?"

"Condenses," I said. "The light condenses the vapor directly from gas to solid, bypassing a liquid state."

"Oh my God," said Lakshmi, "that might work. Shit, that could fucking work. So that means—"

"Instantly—like super instantly condensing to solid," I said, "back to gas when switched, then back to solid."

"Instantly, yes," said Luis, "but with, what you call? Delay, overlap?"

"Latency?" said Lakshmi.

"Yes." Luis clapped. "So you see as laser is switchy-switchy back-forth between these physical state—"

"—it forms the impossible object—" said Lakshmi.

"—at once existing in two states of physical matter," I said.

"Yes, you do see, mis amados, lo imposible es posible. Together we will form the impossible."

They laughed. I laughed. And the giddiness lasted a while longer while we congratulated each other. It felt good. Then an annoying inner voice interrupted to point out that Ranger would too be going all "switchy-switchy" along with the condensed aluminum. I tried to picture it and failed. Imaginations can be merciful that way.

Later that day, as Luis and crew mounted the lasers, I found Ranger at his desk sketching ideas for posters designed to commemorate the event incorporating his jaggy-weird figures.

"Ranger, put that down for a minute, man."

He looked up.

"I want you to close your eyes and try to locate the eensy-weensy part of your brain that has some semblance of self-preservation instinct left intact, and when you've found it, read this."

I gave him a page from my notebook on which I'd scrawled a brief description of the experiment. The final paragraph read:

"The subject will then take his position within the space, both surrounded and intersected by the impossible figure. He will likely experience a tag-along effect from the shifting quantum states, thereby for a period of time—perhaps as long as a few seconds—lose his single-state moorings, or one might say be freed from the determinism that observation plays on an object. During this episode in time, and possibly for an indefinite period thereafter, the subject may experience an indeterminate number of trajectories in potential pathways through cause and effect."

"OK," he said when done reading.

"Any questions?"

"A thousand, but as I've said repeatedly, I prefer not to know."

"You apparently know enough to design prints that someone who survives you will make ridiculous money on. Do you have any heirs? Maybe a sister somewhere who might want to sell those when all but a single version of you in some unreachable dimension vaporizes or folds into pleats or whatever?"

Something big fell in the gym down the hall, probably a ladder. He looked off toward the sound of Luis's reprimands.

"Oh, while I have you," he said, "my publicist is planning out the invitation list. We've honed it down to fifty-five, but if there are any—"

"Fifty-five what?"

He brought his eyes back. "I don't want a circus. Just eight from the press—very selective—then collectors, gallery people, a handful of prominent artists and whomever you might—"

"That's not happening. I'll be the entire audience. Lakshmi and Luis know they need to leave the room, and none of the crew will be there. The occurrence is predicated on having an observer present without whom nothing can, well, occur. The experiment would be complicated geometrically by the presence of more than one observer. We start with just me for the first experiment to establish a base line, then maybe add people one at a time thereafter, assuming there is a thereafter for you—thereafter."

He thought for a moment. "OK, we'll set up video. The audience can watch from down the hall."

"Also a really bad idea. We'll record it and play it for them later, or maybe we can do a tape delay, but I'll have to consider that."

He nodded and started drawing again. "I do in fact have three sisters and a number of nieces and nephews. I believe the number is eight at present. So yes—heirs."

"Will they miss you?"

He lowered his chin and scratched the back of his head. "I can't say. I can't concern myself with that. I have to ask what point you're making."

I took my notebook page back and wrote out another paragraph at the bottom, followed by a signature line.

Ranger read it out loud. "Yes, I fucking understand and I'm too fucking obsessed with my own self-importance to back out now, but I do not in any way hold Oscar responsible, or anyone else for that matter. Anything that happens to me is my own stupid fault."

He signed with his litho crayon, handed it back, and went on with his drawing.

Luis primed the array for the first time on a Sunday night, five weeks and two days after construction began. Ranger was due back the next afternoon, following a week of reflection in an undisclosed location.

Luis tested the system by degrees, toggling on each of the eight main circuits one at a time, then in combination, checking the individual and compound loads. He wasn't happy with the outcome. After six hours of troubleshooting, he and Parker took time to rebuild a couple of connections and recalibrate the scopes while the rest of us got some shuteye. Then they woke us and we repeated the step-by-step procedure. This time, no hitches.

Over fresh coffee and breakfast tostadas, we challenged each other, trying to identify loose ends. Satisfied, we voted to deploy the full load, nods and grins all around.

The power-up began with a hollow sputter followed by a set of thunderous ka-chunks as the series of relays made contact. Before other sounds were heard, though, we felt a buzz transferring up from the floorboards, tickling our soles and shins, then setting our nether-hairs dancing. Just as our rib cages felt like they would start emitting xylophone tones, a super deep frequency hum dropped over us, like the mother of all organ pipes.

We heard a kind of crystalline-cellophane crackle. Then the lasers ignited with a victorious, avian screech that commanded the baritone hum into submission. The lasers seemed to light simultaneously, but in fact fired in tandem in a clockwise direction. If you fluttered your eyelids you could strobe yourself an image of the pattern in progress.

The Necker cube formed at once, but could only be rendered visible by suspending something in the atmosphere that it could illuminate. We tried evaporating dry ice and fanning the vapor into the path of the light beams, which revealed the figure, but only in swirly segments. We moved on to fine particulates—chalk dust, talc powder.

By the end of the fourth day and three dozen trials in, we found a satisfying solution in positioning ourselves in a circle around the figure and blowing pot smoke toward the center, admiring the magnificent, impossible object seemingly materializing from our collective breath.

Convinced that the lasers were doing their jobs, we broke for what we expected would be a day but turned into nearly three, to prepare to test the virtual substrate.

It goes without saying that you don't want to inhale vaporized aluminum, and yet with all our other concerns, that realization didn't hit us until late in the process. As an afterthought, Luis's crew rigged up a "containment superstructure"—outer scaffolding draped with heavy gauge plastic. They sealed it tight and installed a zipper door that you could work from outside or in.

We did a side test of the vapor sprayers in a small containment tent and saw how awful the substance would be to work with. Without the lasers to catalyze the jump-transition to solid form, the vapor condensed into liquid, coated all surfaces, and dripped to the floor.

We sat and considered the mess.

Amber carried some beers over and passed them around.

"You thinking what I'm thinking?" I asked Luis.

He accepted his can with his head still back, staring at the ceiling. "I thinking first we need to try firing laser in this test tent with the vapor but—shit, no, will never work."

"No, it won't. You need the full Necker figure to catalyze the vapor directly into a solid form. There's no point in a test that doesn't involve the fully calibrated Necker cube figure present."

"Yes, right, is too what I am thinking."

We looked to Lakshmi.

"Wait. Hell, no, you can't," she said. "You want to go straight to the performance without properly testing the virtual substrate? That's nuts. You're sending Ranger straight into the fucking unknown."

Luis held up his hand to stop her. He sent Ty, Amber, and Porter out of the gym.

"Ranger will make this decision," he whispered once the door closed behind them, "and I can tell you surely, for Ranger, this is exactly what he want. He insist he be included in the full first implement. Is historical necessity. This right here is him—this fucking unknown—this is his art. This is what makes him great as the artist he is."

"But come on," said Lakshmi, "this is beyond irresponsible."

We stared at our hands for a while.

Then I went for it. "OK, I'll be the one to say it. We have to test the theorem before it gets out there. This is too important to hand off to a bunch of government dipshits to bury in some underground crypt for the next half century while they weigh all the weaponizing options. This is the way it's got to go. So I disagree. This is the most responsible course. This is what history needs from us. It's got to go Ranger's way. I'm with Ranger and history."

Lakshmi took a guzzle of beer, then another.

I said, "Maybe the history thing was a bit over the top."

"No, you're right," she said. "We should prep the sprayers and get Ranger back down here. It's only a matter of time before someone gets wind of this."

I relit the pipe for Lakshmi. We were on the floor, backs to the folded bleachers. From the far side of the gym, we could hear Ranger and Luis, hidden from view by the scaffolding, working out contingencies for the other projects they had underway in New York and Miami.

Lakshmi shuddered as she exhaled.

"Don't do that," I said.

She coughed and dabbed at the corner of her eye with her cuff. She took another short toke before handing the pipe back.

"I know we can't know," she said, "but you must have imagined what's going to happen to him."

"I can't. Instead keep thinking about something Micky said."

She turned to me. "Micky?"

"Yeah, about the evolutionary imperative."

"Micky?"

"Micky said the universe has a need to become godlike. He said that human evolution is the universe's way of learning how to become self-aware, so, you know, through us, the universe gains consciousness and becomes God."

"Micky?"

"I don't think I like what this weed is doing to you."

"So Micky thinks— You're thinking we're going to make Ranger into a god?"

"I would hate myself if I answered yes to that."

"What will Ranger see?"

I took the pipe back.

"Let's try this." I did a countdown in my best mission control voice and launched the pipe high over our heads.

Lakshmi gasped like she was surfacing from underwater and watched it flip end over end, scattering orange sparks and ash. She dove sideways to avoid the fallout, kicking me in the thigh for leverage.

The bronze pipe clattered to the floor.

She lay crumpled. "What the fuck?"

"So," I said, "what did you just observe? Let us consider that the pipe's trajectory was dependent on a broad range of variables: mass, atmospheric density, gravitational acceleration, drag coefficient, propulsive thrust—if you'll excuse the expression. And yet, it flew, tumbled, and returned to earth in just the particular way that you observed. Given slight alterations in the variables, and given all the possible combinations of alternate variables, the pipe might have taken an untold number of paths. And you and I know that untold is a lot."

"So I've been told."

"It's not like any of those thousands of other versions had a lesser chance at existence. They all had potential—like a class full of eager freshman, given a chance, any could have gone on to—"

"I get it."

"Right. So in theory—a theory we will soon test—multiple versions of the incident in which Lakshmi is observing different versions of the pipe-launched-into-space occurrence do indeed take place—potentially speaking."

"But each is mutually exclusive."

"Right. In each version Lakshmi is observing, unaware of any other versions. You are strictly limited in your perceptions, no offense intended. Were we to spread your consciousness wide open—again, no offense intended—you might observe all states and, thereby, all versions would occur for real."

I retrieved the bowl and dipped it in the baggy for a refill.

Lakshmi sat up. "You're thinking Ranger will be open to them all," she said, "all the potential states—multiple versions."

"Yes. Can we picture what that will be like for him? All the versions overlapping at once? Could you imagine a dozen versions of the trajectory of the pipe and our corresponding reactions? A thousand? Our brains aren't built for that. I can't even comb my hair and breathe at the same time. But yes, Ranger will experience them all."

"Whether his brain is capable or not."

"Seems to me, there's a pretty high likelihood it will render his brain incapable of doing anything ever again."

"Or he'll learn to deal with it and become God."

"Again, that thought makes me hate myself. But this could be where evolution is taking us—blowing out our consciousness in this way. If that's possible, we could offer the universe an omniscient view, one worthy of a god. If we can do that, hat's off to Micky."

She slumped and closed her eyes. "And maybe all the thousands of versions will merge into one. Maybe we'll totally fuck with quantum potentialities. Maybe cause and effect will turn inside out."

"Sauce and defect?"

"Maybe it'll do us in, and the universe with it."

"Could happen," I said.

"Then again, maybe this magnificent merging is what humanity has always sought after. Maybe it's the determinism we need—the unified vision—a single path to a perfect world."

She looked up at me.

"Don't worry," I said. "I won't tell anyone you said magnificent merging."

I relit the pipe.

Luis's commands echoed down the hall like dog barks in an alleyway. For the third time, he was demanding silence from Ranger's audience, corralled in the jerry-rigged control room at the front of the school. The lot of them were collectively incensed at being denied the privilege of witnessing even a replay of the performance.

Luis supported me in the decision to remove the video camera from the gym because, remote or otherwise, we couldn't risk having more than one observer. Ranger's guests we decided would have to be satisfied with being in close proximity to the historic event. Ranger, being deep into his pre-performance self-immersion, was passive on the matter.

Ultimately, on threat of removal, the crowd hushed. I watched Luis round the corner at the end of the darkened hallway, a bulldog back lit by the lobby windows, shadow stretching nearly to my position by the gym door. His footfalls beat like a countdown. "Go Ty," he called out. "Now, now, kick it on!"

He gave me a thumbs up and returned to the control room.

I felt more than heard the chunk of the ignition relay and waited until the familiar murmur rose from the floor. I went back into the gym where the lacquered boards were singing a cicada chorus. I tapped Ranger's photographer on the shoulder to let her know her time was up. She stooped and fired off a few more of Ranger and Lakshmi positioned about five yards from the containment structure.

"But you don't have to go through with this to make your precious art, do you?" Lakshmi was nose to nose with Ranger, she standing, he sitting on his soon to be insanely valuable, autographed piano stool.

"Isn't it art enough to have taken the project to this point?" she said. "We'll send a box turtle in there and you can draw some damn pictures and write some free verse."

Ranger's eyes were closed. He was clothed in his blue terrycloth robe and fucking scarf. "I know this is upsetting to you, but no, it would not be art. It wouldn't even be parody. It would be nothing."

"But we've already achieved epoch-making, breakthrough shit here. You will be in the history books as the patron who underwrote this experiment."

The vibration was building. My earlobes quivered.

Ranger smiled and held his hands out. His fingers blurred at the edges with the vibrations. He looked at me. "How long?"

"You should come on over."

Lakshmi's face was red. She wiped her nose on the back of her hand, turned for the door, pivoted back, hugged Ranger around the neck, and released him with a shove, sending him for a full clockwise revolution on his stool.

"Watch it, man," I said to him. "You don't want to get any taller."

He failed in his attempt to smile.

We walked toward the containment tent entrance. One of his knees wobbled. He wavered, but kept his back straight, leaning forward to firm his stride. We stopped just short of the entrance.

I unzipped the opening and turned to Ranger just as the bass hum overwhelmed us.

His eyes were wide and glazed. The vibrations loosed a tear that slid to his chin, and as he saw me notice, he parted his robe, pulled it off, and folded it over his arm.

His entire naked form was out of focus with the hum.

I took the robe. I had to scream over the crackling lasers. "You're looking kind of blurry, man. You OK?"

He nodded with overcompensating vigor.

"Because if you have to puke, we'll power down and try another—"

"I'm fine, Oscar."

Luis's blue lights flashed overhead, our thirty-second signal.

My mouth was spitless. I didn't think my tongue would work. "I don't understand the art," I shouted, "but I want to say—"

He shook his head.

"I said, I don't get the art, but I understand why you have to do it."

He smiled for real, and in a single physics-defying motion, slipped a finger into the knot of his scarf and removed it.

He stepped close. "If you understand the need to do it, you understand the art. It's one and the same."

He hung the scarf around my neck and kept his hands there, pressing his knuckles into my chest. "It's OK, Oscar. Death is not a frightening thing. I learned that from you."

"From me?"

He put his lips to my ear. "You lying there near death in the back of your van—laid out to perfection, arms arranged over your chest. Looking like the lid of an alabaster sarcophagus."

"In the van! What the fuck? You said you weren't there."

The hum eased.

"You were dead. You were at peace. But then you came back and committed that reprehensible act. In death, there are no questions, no blame. In death, there is a return to the unquestioned reason that unites all things."

The blue flashing lights went solid. From behind me, I could hear the vaporizers charging. The lasers squawked on at a painful volume.

"You lying bastard!" My voice was failing me. "Why didn't you tell me you were there?"

He released the scarf. "Thank you, Oscar."

He stepped past me and through the opening.

CHAPTER FIVE

In which Ranger attempts to document in verse another version of Oscar's death.

Shuddery, stone cold.

No, that's not right. It's a metallic cold.

Shuddery, shaky, body-quaky, meat locker cold.

How to say, feeling cold and yet not feeling? The shivers, but without the sting.

Am I filling space? Am I displacing air? I'm here, but not here, and yet the crackling when I inhale—ice crystals forming on my nostril hairs.

Crackling nasal follicles.

Nostricles.

Ha!

Tiny crinkle-clinks.

Tinkly-ice, stalactite nostril-cave clinkers.

Good, good. That's good.

The vaguest of light is passing through the windshield. The street lights are all out. Unlit lights. Dull city light. It's radiating from, it seems, nowhere.

From lit-less lights, dull, orangy-gray not-quite light.

Bah.

Dull-lit-city

Look at Oscar, dead asleep, and soon dead.

Oscar's breath in the air, roiling.

Oscar-breath roiling into the stale air.

Breath-billows in the orangy-gray windshield light.

But gah, the gas fumes.

Gas fumes rising with the Oscar-breath.

The cold bears down, like doom descending.

Oh God, that's awful.

The cold worries down the Oscar-musty-fume clouds.

"Fess up, fucker!"

From outside, the argument, like ice picks stabbing at the wall of the van.

Voice-clatter, all kit-a-braah. Braaaa. Rat-a-braah.

Their boots grinding the salt crystals on the black-frozen street.

Boots a-crackle, circling, whetstone grinding.

In here, thick air—the old gas can is in the corner behind Oscar.

In these shadows, a gas can fumes.

The shadows consume the fumes.

Fume-a-sume.

Oh, now, that's truly awful.

Let's move along with this. "Oscar. Hey. You need to wake up, Oscar."

Oscar, the curled cur, hands between thighs.

Dogs don't have hands. Thighs, questionable as well.

Oscar, caterpillar curled.

His cheek raw to the bare floor. That ribbed, frozen, scratch-rusted metal floor.

The orangy-greyness lights Oscar's one exposed eye and that soft cheekbone.

Below his eyelid, the thin, gentle fold.

What sensitivity he has, inscribed in that fold, a frozen salt trail licking the outer corner.

The mildewed moving blanket encases him like a cocoon. Oscar, it's stiffened on you.

Mildew-stiffened frozen crust.

A frozen cast.

Mildew-frosted shroud.

A wet crackle from your throat. A sharp inhale. There you go, Oscar, at last. Loll your head. Open your eyes. Yes, Oscar, the Ill-fated, the argument is stirring you.

"Oscar! Awaken!"

Oscar sucks in five-degree air. Wheezing, he squeezes his eyes tighter, coughing.

"Come on, now, open your eyes, Oscar." There you go. Find me—those irreverent green eyes.

Oscar is looking up. He speaks.

"Big." He coughs. "Whoa. Damn, you're..." Gags. "Damn, you're big. Damn, so drunk."

"Yes, you drank Oscar. You took something, as well." How must I look here, hunched over Oscar, barely contained by the van?

I'm sitting. I'm fitting.

To fit, I must sit.

Oscar is squinting. "What the— Who? Who are the fuck are you? Ghost giant."

"No." I like that. But no.

"I can see right through you."

"Rather trite, Oscar. I've never tried to hide my ambitions."

"What? No, the light's through— The light's coming through you. Are you here?"

Sigh. "Ah, that's the question. If I could only answer simply, Oscar."

"You're not real."

"Yes, I am, but I can't answer that simply."

"I'm an engine..." Cough. "I'm a fucker...ing engineering physics major, man."

"I know, Oscar. But I'm not a scientist and even if I were—well, you won't be alive long enough for an explanation."

"Funny. And why're you so damn big?"

The screaming outside—"You didn't fucking fuck her?"—hitting its crescendo. Forte. Fortissimo. "You're lying. You cowardly bastard. You lying bastard!"

Fortississimo!

"What are they—" Oscar looks toward the shouts. "What's happening out there?"

I bend way down to Oscar's ear. "My size and the transparency and so forth, it's a distortion I think—a little different with each variant of tonight. And with many of the versions, I'm more solid. And some versions occurred a bit earlier, so I know what's coming, or what may come, depending on how this version plays out."

"You're a trip, man."

"In one version you say something about it being 'an anomaly of the isolated quantum system.' And then something concerning 'decoherence.' What does that mean, Oscar? Can you tell me if I'll get free from this, whatever this is?"

Oscar laughs. He wheezes some more. "Versions of tonight? Oh, man, I bet you're fun at a party."

"Yes, yes, Oscar. You were with me at the party."

"Was I? Would I? Could I?"

Oscar's voice is dry frost. It's useless, getting anything out of that addled brain.

The voices outside are bashing at each other.

Clangor-shouts, maces on armor.

"What're they saying?" Oscar lifts his head. "Why's he so pissed?"

I try blowing out some air. My breath doesn't show. An anomaly for sure.

"Jealous rage, Oscar. He's green with rage. OK, quick summary, because you don't have long: Mr. Green is interrogating your friend."

"Micky?"

"Yes, Micky Green is at odds with—name escapes me. Anyway, Nameless Friend is suspected of having had sex earlier this evening with Micky Green's woman friend, possibly in this van or possibly at her apartment. It's irrelevant—that is, to my predicament."

"Tookie? He's yelling at Tookie?" Oscar cracks the blanket off his shoulder. Twists. "Shit, why am I so fucked up?" Rolls back.

"You took a narcotic, Oscar."

"Oh God, the Nembutal." Eyes rolling, fluttering.

"Look at me for a second. Oscar? Oscar?"

"What?"

"Would you say that it's as cold as a meat locker in here?"

"What?"

"Cold as a what? What would you say?"

"Witch's tit."

"No, that won't do. And one more: what would the word 'nostricle' mean to you?"

A thump, heavy, rocks us both.

Oscar shakes his lovely head. "Fuck? Who's hitting my van?"

The screams are muffled by pain sounds.

Growl-swallowed screams.

"Your friend outside—Tookie—is being beaten by the jealous Micky Green. He's being thrown against the side of your van."

Oscar jerks his head to the side, trying to right himself. "Tookie? Tookie." Throws his head upward but nothing follows.

"Tookie, yes, your bloody friend, Tookie. Tookie, Tookie, Tookie. Your friend, Tookie, is being killed."

"Fu—uuck. I can't get up." Oscar succeeds in turning over. Collapses onto his face.

"Here's the rest of it, Oscar: Your extremities are numb from exposure. You were passed out for nearly three hours in this horrid cold.

Three interminable hours I've waited."

Clanks. We hear metal scraping and nick-clinking the side of the van. More pounding.

Pound for pound, clink for clank.

Oscar is hissing with effort. "My damn legs. They're dead. Am I going to lose my legs?"

"It doesn't matter. They'll work well enough for what comes next."

Oscar drops to his shoulder. He's looking up at me. "What next? What? Well enough for what?"

"You're not going to be alive much longer. A few minutes. A minute."

Outside, a scream, snapped off.

"Oh, my God, what's he doing to Tookie?"

Clang, against the street. Resolves to ringing.

Oscar drops his face into the blanket, huffing. Slobber-huffs. "Oh G—od."

"That was the the bludgeoning weapon hitting the pavement. Micky Green has just finished killing your friend."

Tomorrow's headline: Green Kills.

Tinny taps at the back door.

"There—hear that? Hear the keys? The killer Green took the van keys from your friend. He'll open the door now."

The key misses, scratching at the back door.

Searchy. Scratchy.

Oscar turns. His eyes—all the sensitivity blown into panic. His cheeks are slick. Breath moisture. Snot.

"Oh, fuck me. Phoenicia."

"Ah, so there you are. Yes, you were with Phoenicia earlier, Killer Green's girlfriend. And Oscar?"

"What? Christ, what?"

"You'll hide under the blanket now."

The key snicks into place.

Oscar's forearms move like numb flippers. This part gets me—the frantic numb-fumbling.

Numbly flippifers.

He flippers the blanket-cast. Covers his head. He balls up behind the driver's seat. Balls caterpillar tight.

Caterpillar-Oscar, ball tight.

Squeeeaak. The back door opens with a squeal.

Tookie's killer is doubled over, shouldering Tookie's corpse. Green squats, then flings. Tookie's body uncoils.

Dead flail, flat back onto the van bare floor.

His head— bang—on the rusty-scratch floor.

Dead-ropy arms flail rubbery against the Oscar-ball.

Tookie's killer is steaming, panting. Breath-pulsing steam. Bare Moses arms, steaming. He bends Tookie's knees. Gives Tookie a shove.

Dead Tookie fits.

For a Hollywood silhouette moment, the killer stands. Shaking, throbbing.

He steps away.

Tookie's blond locks are green-white in the throw of orangy-gray light, braided black with blood.

Gummy frozen blacky-blood and eye-pooly.

Gummy pool of blacky-blood fills an eye, over-woven by a tarred snake tangle.

Moan. Oh my, how Mr. Green moans. He's back at the door, his steam thinning. He tosses the bludgeoning, clank-weapon. It pops off Tookie's belly, clatters to the rusty-scratch metal.

People, let me tell you, it's an iron fire bar.

It's an iron in the fire.

A tire bar.

It's a tire iron, people.

Killer Green is still at the door.

Steamy-thin frozen air.

Steam killer.

The door, grr-aack, squeals. He slams the door.

Boot-crackle footsteps circling. The driver door opens. Killer Green climbs up, drops leaden into the seat. Beats at the wheel. Screeches like a widow. Double-fists the wheel. Whines like a kitten. Keys the engine on. Revs.

Shrieks like a widow.

The motor roars, then gurgles down, rumbly beneath us. Oscar is whispering.

Oscar hisses 'neath the rumbly.

I know, I know, Oscar-pillar. But you have to uncoil, my dear, fool genius. Uncoil and rise.

I put my mouth to the blanket. "Oscar, in there? You'll use the tire iron."

The van revs higher. We're rocked back, thrown back. The tires a-crunch on the crust.

Tires grind the road-ice-crunchy.

Oscar rolls open, freeing himself in Tookie's dead, rubber arms.

The van jumps ahead, then angles hard over an ice bump, flipping Oscar, frozen trout in a griddle.

Oscar lands belly down over Tookie's tar-pooly face. He flippers for the tire iron. Fumbles it in, crooks it in his elbows.

Oscar rolls up to his knees.

A hard turn, opposite. Oscar topples, head clunking the wall.

Killer Green wrenches to his right to see us. But that's the wrong way to see us. Oscar is crouching low, Mr. Killer.

Killer turns back. Sobs. Pummels the wheel. Yanks at the wheel, shaking.

Pity the wheel.

He punches the van faster. Rounds a curve wide, pinning Oscar to the wall.

And, oh yes, here we go, the wide boulevard, confused with traffic.

Past diamond strung street lamps.

Past streaking glinties.

Faster still, the Killer wailing, speeds faster, pawing his eyes.

Wailing between lanes, blind with glinty-streaks passing.

No point in whispering now. I'll belt it out. "Now, Oscar! You'll use it now, Oscar."

Oscar's up, tire iron crooked in his elbows. He steps out to the right and swings left.

Swing-falls left.

He falls into his swing.

The tire iron spears Green's nose-bridge. Rips him a new nose.

Unspeakable scream.

Killer thrashes. He leg-a-jerks out, flooring the pedal. The engine roars, vengeful.

The van hooks left into the traffic. We're hurled right.

I call out. "It's happening now, Oscar! It's now."

A silent second, then—

The first car kisses us.

The second misses us.

The third bites us, spins us.

The fourth ignites us.

The fifth one ends us.

CHAPTER SIX

We read passages from Lakshmi's lab diary documenting the events leading up to the August 30th impossible figure incident.

FEB 20 :

Odd art fellow, goes by Ranger (rhymes with banger). Corners me outside my fourth 1410 class in two days. I'm so, so beat. Incapable of exhibiting interest. This Ranger—otherworldly. Also tenacious, insufferable. Far too tall. Far too styled. Way too white.

> **Me:** And why exactly does an artist do a fellowship in the physics department?
> **Him:** I expect you can tell me that.

Wants to chat about "existential theories." Looking to establish his project objectives.

> **Me:** Can you explain what you're asking for, since I'm not getting a sense of it?

Him: No, I wouldn't want to do that , even if I could. Exploring realms beyond my understanding or even capacity to understand is at the heart of my process.

Me: My process starts with a hypothesis. You might try that instead.

Turn for my escape. Pray he can recognize a blowoff when he sees one.

FEB 22 :

Second Oddfellow encounter occurs at fatuous undergrad kegger. Took refuge in kitchen.

Determined to wait for Delia just to give her shit for insisting I meet her there. Instead, maddeningly gifted undergrad-gone-AWOL Oscar Hiller appears. Smug, snide, reticent, condescending. Under influence of substance(s) rendering him zoned, wild-eyed, diagonally skewed. Demonstrating unquenchable thirst for life-endangering punch. Somehow charming in a way wise to disregard, as per several women on campus.

Ranger appears. Inexplicable. Studies Oscar's behavior like an entomologist. Oscar absorbs himself in my Escher book. Add psychotropics to Oscar's suspected drug regimen. Oscar's mind whirring in physically evident way re: Escher drawing. His questions suggest he's three steps ahead of me theory-wise. Cheeky, undeserving, self-entitled twerp. Cute though, damn me.

Oscar and Ranger have words re: Oscar's disdain vis-à-vis Ranger's profession. Ranger undeterred. Captivated by Oscar's absorption in Escher's Ascending and Descending.

Oscar stands, wavers in manner as if to illustrate his understanding of how simultaneous Ascending/Descending might occur, then overcome by sudden purge impulse. Lunges for exit, tips punchbowl, dousing me as fond fare-thee-well.

Attempt my own exit but must deal with Ranger the Relentless.

> **Ranger:** What is a Penrose triangle?
> **Ranger:** Can you explain the connection between Escher's art and quantum physics?
> **Ranger:** What is the nature of your current project?
> **Ranger:** Do you have a patron?

Patron?

Meanwhile, I'm a-drip with caustic red swill.

> **Me:** Oscar may in fact be formulating his quantum perception hypothesis down there in the alley. Perhaps you should question him further.

Ranger pursues Oscar.

Blot at jeans with mildewed kitchen sink mat, head home. Sopping attire, near-zero temps. Find Delia at home, clueless. Thank her for another fab'lous Sat'day nigh (lips numb).

FEB 23 :

Early, Delia returns to bedroom and wakes me.

In state of high drama re: news of a student's horrid van accident somehow connected to murder of local boy. Murder suspect, also townie, near death from gruesome burns. Student said to be largely intact. Something about frostbite.

For remainder of day head echoing with self-lecturing re: failure to see Oscar home from the party. Thinking I should visit Oscar at the hospital.

I don't.

FEB 26 :

Again, Ranger waiting to pounce outside 1410 classroom, pressing for Oscar's address.

Me: St. Vincent's.

Him: I've been there. He's been released. Do you have his home address?

Me: No.

After 4:20 class, head to Oscar's apartment with quart of dining hall fish chowder. Door ajar. Oscar stretched out on couch, foot elevated, ballooned with bandages.

Me: Brilliant work. Does it hurt?

Him: You know that they removed two of my toes, right?

Me: Would you prefer I feign sympathy or call you an imbecile for getting atomically wasted and crawling into the back of your van to die of exposure?

Him: Let's go with the feigning. Why are you here?

Strewn about are fragments of his scribbled formula on paper plates, newspaper margins, paycheck stub.

Me: Would you like me to bring you a notebook?

Him: No, but you can bring me some water for this lovely, big ass Percocet, yum?

I comply.

Oscar without pretext launches into nonsensical story involving Ranger the Odd in the van. Exhibits difficulty distinguishing between memories and nightmares that plagued him in the hospital. To the effect of: captivity in freezing van, abstruse conversation with Ranger, murderous shouts, a shadowy assailant, Ranger singing out in free verse as van spins out of control, etc.

Describes Ranger's "semi-present state."

We explore the notion, also referenced by Oscar as "materially non-definitive." He posits Ranger's translucency may be metaphor for a transient state— between multi-verses.

Me: I saw Ranger. He didn't mention being in the van with you.
O: Yeah, I can see him keeping that to himself.
Me: Why?
O: A person was murdered.
Me: Ah. And, just curious, pretentious though he may be, why would Ranger happen to be mid-transition between multiverses?
O: No clue. (Eyes dart to his formula scrawls.) But I'm not saying he was transitioning. I said he was a metaphor for a transitional state. Ranger's just the type of guy you need for a good metaphor. In your room full of average Joes, he'd be the most likely candidate for quantum transition metaphor, don't you think?
Me: I can't imagine what Ranger is good for. Just explain to me why one would need such a metaphor? How about this instead— you're remembering a dream, which makes sense because dreams are metaphorical, even if most dream metaphors are just rubbish, your psyche tossing nonsense by the wayside as it wrestles with guilt and anxiety.
O: These weren't dreams, no. Never have dreams like that.
Me: You're probably feeling guilty for being bitchy to Ranger, and with the trauma and all, you experienced a big time guilt and anxiety nightmare.

O: Oh that's really rich. I'm feeling guilty about giving Ranger a well-deserved dose of derision? My friend was just killed, largely as a result of my stupidity, and you're thinking the trauma was triggered by guilt over hurting Ranger's feelings?

Me: Shit. Right, I'm sorry. It's very sad. How do you feel about—"

O: It wasn't a fucking dream. It wasn't fully real, but I can distinguish a fucking dream from an alternate state of consciousness. And I was conscious and I was seriously altered.

Me: OK, sorry. So tell me why is your alternate state experience full of metaphors?

O: (Faraway gaze, designed to look fetching.) Reality is essentially metaphorical, just like dreams. We create models in our minds for everyday stuff, like chairs. It makes a chair easy to identify when you come upon one. We're so conditioned to it, we take the metaphors at face value. Have you ever really looked at a tree? It's a freaky big plant, like science fiction freaky. Don't you think trees are referencing deeper meanings? There's gotta be more going on there. What's a tree mean?

(Steady gaze.)

Me: Oh, was that a question?

O: Unanswerable, but yes.

Me: I've never heard you talk this way, Oscar. You're normally the first to snicker when science devolves into metaphysical claptrap.

O: Ah, you're disappointed in me.

Me: You can do better. Your brain can do better.

O: Maybe I had an awakening. Maybe being nearly damn dead did that to me— revelations of Maya or something spiritual-ly and Hindu-y. I don't know. Check with your people.

Me: My people would say, you should get back to your studies.

He pouted for a bit. Asked/ordered me to adjust the space heater. Asked/ordered me to heat up his soup for him.

Upon return from kitchen, find him assembling the paper scraps in proper order. His formula includes spacial coordinates that want to bridge to the 4th, maybe 5th dimension. Ask if he's trying to describe a Necker cube.

> **O:** Well, yeah. Isn't it obvious?
> **Me:** Do you want me to give Ranger your address?
> **O:** Negative. (Holds up finger.) Wait. Wait. Yes-sssss, I think the Percs are kicking in. (Closes eyes.)

He asks for his soup. I prop the bowl on his chest.

> **O:** (Spooning soup with eyes shut.) Chef Inge loves me. (slurp) Makes this special for me. (slurp, slurp) Crew at the dining hall asking about me?
> **Me:** No. (a lie) Shall I bring more soup tomorrow?
> **O:** See if she'll do the navy bean and bacon.
> **Me:** Need anything else before I go?
> **O:** Maybe a cuddle.

I leave.

MARCH 12:

Ranger is five minutes early for his officially scheduled and therefore unavoidable appointment at my department office. Announces he's endowed Oscar with a grant to pursue his theorem. Setting him up at "off-campus facility," generous funding, etc. Wants me to work for him for duration of project.

I tell him:

a) already working on a related hypothesis;

b) pretty sure his offer would violate my graduate scholarship agreement;

c) pretty sure he has no clue how to conduct an efficacious research project or the need for such;

d) pretty sure Oscar lacks the maturity to take his theorem anywhere meaningful.

He says c) and d) are why he needs me.

Offer to get him in touch with the Emerson-Dargis Institute people if he wants to fund a legit research project. Says that sort of oversight would subvert his process. Offers me $15k per month for a minimum of three months to keep Oscar on track.

I hush him. Walk him to Roman Town Pizza to continue.

Ranger downs three sausage and pepper slices while I think.

Agrees to my stipulations to: a) stay clear of university; b) keep mum on what transpires; c) heed my ethical guidance; d) grant me option of being cited in research findings—or (importantly) not.

Me: Can you first lay out the goals of the project so we're clear?
Him: The art is both the process and the objective. All serves the art. Can I have your answer please? (Stands.)
Me: OK, as long as Oscar doesn't know about the stipend.
Him: Agreed. An NDA will be forthcoming.

MARCH 13:

Delia takes news I'll be tutoring Oscar evenings (a lie) not well. Calls me a "fuck-awful half-truther." Realize her trash talk is what once turned me on about her.

I plead for forbearance. Takes that not well too.

> **Me:** Yes, it's not really and totally about tutoring Oscar, but that's all I can say.
> **Delia:** Since when am I expected to tolerate you being a duplicitous bitch?
> **Me:** Since I'm doing shit I'm getting paid well to keep secret?
> **Delia:** (glare)
> **Me:** And it's for your own good.

Stomps into bedroom. Sulks. Returns. Peppers me with Oscar-related questions. On and on till I semi-lose my shit and call her clingy and pre-menstrual. Stomps back to bedroom for coat, and then out. Stays with I'm guessing Beatrice for night.

APRIL 20:

Check arrives from RangArt, LLC for $15k. I've done nary shit to earn anything yet. Have had no contact with Oscar nor a Ranger sighting in weeks.

Track down Ranger at his posh but threadbare-around-the-edges hotel. He's cleared a wall of hotel art and taped up a grid of darkroom proofs—daily progression of Oscar's formula. Asks me to look it over and leaves for the night. Order shrimp salad sandwich, iced tea, rice pudding from room service.

Study formula till wee hours. Good start. OK, impressive start. Solid footings. Lacks focus, yet lays groundwork for at least a dozen possible paths forward, half at least heading for dead-ends. One or two might work out, but many holes, some definitely unfillable.

He'll need me soon, or he'll lose faith and quit. Leave note to that effect for Ranger.

APRIL 26:

Return to Ranger's hotel room looking for updates. Not present.

MAY 10:

Ditto

MAY 24:

Note in my box from Ranger, orange crayon on sketch paper:

> "You will work tonight. Will pick you up at 6:00 at your apt. Make yourself look nice."

Dig out cousin Rajiv's tattered football hoodie from the hamper and ink-stained, baggy-ass sweatpants, bind my hair and wait out front.

Ranger arrives. Enjoy his disapproving squint.

The "facility:" dark, derelict school. Like crypt where ghosts of students endlessly repeat Calculus II. Oscar's classroom smells sour in multiple dimensions: pot-smoke-sock-fart-onion-dip-stale-beer.

But

oh

my

god

the

formula.

Before can get my head into it, a moment of vertigo. Overcome by his chalk lines. Loops, expressions, gestures. Oscar the choreographer.

What I want to say in that moment: Oh, Oscar, Oscar, Oscar.
What I say: This clause is unconvincing.
Oscar: Unconvincing to you or to the scientific community?
Me: To me.
Oscar: Damn. OK.

Simple fix, fairly simple. Another few hours to nudge him back in line. A realignment.

Done.

Ranger heads out for the night.

Oscar hobbles out of classroom sometime after whining on about residual toe pain. Returns in hash-induced haze.

Refuse toke but accept Genesee. Another.

Me: Don't you miss people in this place?
Him: Ranger is people, in a vague sense. He keeps me company.
Me: So can brooms.
Him: No. My answer is no.

Me: You don't really recognize the essential connection between people, do you?

Him: I believe there is something that binds us together. It's thick and so strong it takes a corrosive solvent to remove it.

Me: You're describing tar.

Oscar nods off.

I sit back, take in the full formula. The visual. The art of it.

Oscar's gentle snoring. An eyelid flutters. The golden bristles gracing his cheeks.

What I want to ask: Oscar, do you recognize the beauty of the formula? Where does it come from, Oscar? What source do you draw from? At what god's feet do you lay your flowers?

Instead, I go.

JUNE 16 :

Arrive at work at 8:15. Two coffees shy of lucidity. Find Ranger's sticky note above my office doorknob. Locate Ranger out in the quad sitting through downpour like despondent squid in tidal pool. Fills me in on Oscar's see-sawing behavior:

1. Oscar works at manic pace, thereby bringing on a hair-on-fire panic attack

2. runs off to self-destructive hookup with Micky Green's poison ivy girlfriend

3. accompanies her to horrid deathbed visit with poor SOB Micky Green

4. returns to school to encounter Ranger creating reflective Necker cube art

5. bing bong—eureka moment—envisions improved path for the formula

6. concurrently, reality check as Ranger imposes draconian deadline for fabricator's CAD/CAM instructions

7. hence Oscar's current hostage-of-his-own-taking situation in the classroom.

Somewhere around #6, experience pang of nausea re: recognition of own denseness.

Me: What fabricator? What does Oscar want to fabricate?
Ranger: Not Oscar, me. The Necker cube.
Me: Oh. But no, that's not—
Ranger: The Necker cube sculpture that I'll climb into during my performance. Oscar, I'm sure, explained about my performance.
Me: Yes, but not really, because you— I mean, you realize that— You can't— You're joking, right?"
Ranger: (prolonged stare) Not intentionally, but then that would be part and parcel of the performance. Certainly, it would not be the desired outcome.

Demand to see Oscar ASAP. Ranger assures me that was his intention, re: #7, Oscar's classroom barricade.

Hurry to Ranger's car. Realize once underway that my 9:15 students will soon assemble in my classroom in my absence.

At the school, some elaborately inked Mexican hit-man-looking dude gets instantly all up in Ranger's business. Thinking R owes money to the wrong sorts until he introduces stranger as Luis, aka El Fabricante.

I attempt classroom ingress. Oscar unresponsive.

Luis continues colorful, multilingual assault on Ranger out front, then vamooses.

Ranger offers me apology (most shocking of day's events). Sends me out with his car to retrieve lunch. In his cargo area find footlocker filled with Ranger-philia—exhibition catalogs, coffee table volumes, art journals. Grab a selection.

Agree with Ranger to wait three hours before re-attempting entry. Killing time, Ranger uses his art books to provide docent's tour of his storied career. Glowingly describes his Berlin outdoor exhibition about six years back—"The Treachery of Images"—a kind of yin-yang dialog between his real and perceived personas.

Me: And I take it you discovered you have a real self?
Ranger: You're being sarcastic.
Me: No.
Ranger: That was sarcasm too, I take it. Your question is not inappropriate. I can't answer it, though. But it was a fabulously reviewed exhibition.
Me: And since that performance, you've been up to what?
Ranger: Two notable exhibits: Vienna; Brooklyn Bridge Park.
Me: Well received?
Ranger: The Vienna Light Selector drew impressive crowds.
Me: And what was the critical reaction?
Ranger: Good.

Me: Good?

Ranger: Fairly good.

Me: And Brooklyn Bridge Park.

Ranger: That was the 1000 Polanski Dicks.

Me: Oh my.

R: There was a crowd control problem.

Me: And the critics?

R: (throat clearing, ear scratching) Any artist that strives to be meaningful to a broad audience becomes a convenient whipping boy for critics. They contend that any work the mass public can appreciate is by its nature too pedestrian to be art.

Me: Berlin was three years ago. You must be in dire need of a hit.

R: (introspective eye-drift) I do performance art. That means, I need an audience, which means I need spectacle, which means I need investor funds. Money is not the objective, it's a tool.

Me: Like a pallet knife.

R: If you like.

Me: And if this new project fails, that will probably kill your bankability for good.

R: It won't.

Me: Investors will still believe in you?

R: It won't fail.

Two plus hours later, take advantage of rain shower to test supposition that no man can refuse a wet female. Gain swift entry via back window.

Fully expect to share some yucks with Oscar re: Ranger's delusion that a material demonstration of the theorem is possible.

I laugh alone.

Oscar admits complicity. Shows me new formula amendment and CAD/CAM projection of same.

> **Me to self:** Still, girl, be real. Oscar can't possibly succeed in formulating Ranger's Necker cube design. Impossible objects are impossible.
> **Self to me:** Oh god, the new formula amendments may not be total bullshit.
> **Me to self:** Even so, seriously, render it into an engineering blueprint? Seriously?
> **Self to me:** The CAD/CAM plan is still impossible, and yet it's about 90% less impossible than I thought possible.

Natural instinct to panic, flee and notify the authorities wrestles with elation over taking part in universe-pretzeling, career-launching theoretical breakthrough.

In self-preservative reflex action accept vodka shot.

Again.

Again.

Come to realize, given my contribution to possibly loosing the under-pinnings of cause and effect in literally unimaginable ways, I bear a responsibility to get my fucking head straight—something only some-one lubed on vodka shots would be foolish enough to think they might manage while, well, lubed on vodka shots. I resort to a sophomore year organizational exercise.

On the board, I draw a Venn diagram titled:

JUST HOW MUCH DO I CARE ABOUT...?

Populate said diagram thusly:

Circle (A) = Ranger

Circle (B) = Oscar

Circle (C) = Delia

Circle (D) = Self

Circle (E) = Universe, inhabitants, et al

My **Oscar** circle **(B)** looms large, disturbingly about 20% bigger than **Universe (E)**, plus the overlap is considerable given Oscar's singular talent for unraveling important things, e.g., civility, relationships, matter, time.

The **Ranger** circle **(A)** is about 40% the area of **Oscar (B)** and overlaps about 30% of same and 10% of **(E)**, because Ranger is little more than a sacrificial pawn in the scheme of things, mostly Oscar's guinea pig. But the prospect of Ranger perishing? Increase his size a bit.

Draw circle **(D)**, aka **me**, about half the size of **Oscar (B)** for reasons I can't explain. And my circle includes the intersections of **(A)**, **(B)**, and **(E)**, while totally eclipsed by their size. In other words, if I let Oscar and Ranger carry on their work unchecked, I'm probably toast— professionally, existentially and so forth.

Delia (C) is a diminutive circle adjacent to mine and, yes, overlapping mine by about 20%. Remove her. Return her at a smaller size.

Since I haven't provided Oscar with a key to the circles, we turn it into a drinking game.

Oscar: OK, I think I've got it. **(A)** is your job, **(B)** is your love life, **(C)** is the good ol' US of A, **(D)** is your dog, **(E)** is the fate of the Universe.

Me: Nope. And how the hell did you know that **(E)** was the fate of the Universe?

Oscar: (drinks) Wow. The bluff pays off. So **(B)** is me, **(D)** is you because you lie to yourself and the world about your own importance, **(A)** is Ranger and **(C)** is your dog, not **(D)**.

Me: I don't have a dog. And that's very sweet. You think I'm more important than I think I am?

Oscar: (drinks) Do you have a lover?

Me: Semi.

Oscar: Then **(C)** is her.

Me: What makes you think it's a she?

Oscar: Oh no, I'm right aren't I?

Me: (drinks)

Oscar is having fun. He requests another diagram:

NOW THAT THE END IS NIGH, I DEARLY REGRET...

Circle (A) = Baby seals, never cuddled

Circle (B) = Mums Rajma Masala sauce, never mastered

Circle (C) = Nobel prize, unwon

Circle (D) = Blues organ, never mastered

Circle (E) = Oscar, re: unrequited in some way perhaps but not necessarily sexually, although whatever

Me: OK, go.

Oscar: **(A)** is your unfulfilled desire to bear children; **(B)** is food-related; **(C)**, given it's puniness, must be some superficial accomplishment like getting your class B learner's permit; **(D)** is playing the blues organ; **(E)** is about love.

He reaches for the shot glass. I slap it to the floor. Inform him I already have my class B driver's license. Ask him what he imagines might happen to Ranger. He summons idiotic analogy: starlings sucked into jet engine.

Argument ensues. Unable to maintain train of thought or, for that matter, consciousness.

Wake hours later beside Oscar.

Wake again sometime thereafter with leg draped over him. Nod off feeling comforted in a way I don't want to consider.

JUNE 17:

Unspoon in nick of time, moments before Oscar wakes.

Leaden head. Tongue like styrofoam.

Ranger drives us to Gold Star Diner. Gut like wrung-out mop, and yet consumed by thoughts of food. All else too painful to contemplate.

Massive order of pancakes, onion rings, sausage. Drown with cheap blueberry syrup. Squirts of hot sauce. Oscar slides mustard beyond my reach.

Post-gorge. Metabolism close to shutting down.

Ranger, no doubt taking full advantage of Oscar's compromised state, presents him with a release form of dubious legal repute.

Oscar's face unreadable.

> **What I want to say:** Why are you even considering this, Oscar? Clearly you recognize the high probability the experiment will kill Ranger. Do you seriously think a sketchy release will absolve you of criminal wrongdoing (AKA murder)?
> **What I say:** Wait. What?

Oscar offers token challenge to Ranger's recklessness. Belches. Signs the release. Wipes up eggy-wegg remains from plate with wheat toast.

I manage some spluttery, half-formed expressions of exasperation re: Ranger using artsy-fartsy pseudo-philosophizing as cover for historically excessive vainglory.

> **Me:** (a sample) What, like, you're envisioning, like what, Ranger? What will come of this? A Necker cube fucking casket, that's what. Your eternal fucking multidimensional tomb. And what're we— Because you realize your body and the cube all intersecting together in ways never before—well, I mean, shit. Do you think you'll just reappear—poppity-pip—from whatever pleat of reality you slip into? Or no, because you won't go anywhere, will you? It'll all be the same-where. It'll just be fucking same-where all at once, forever. This is nuts."
> **Ranger:** Same-where. That will be useful for my artist's statement. My biggest challenge will be representing the event in a way people can comprehend.
> **Me:** That's not even close to your biggest challenge. And comprehension? Ha! You're absolving yourself of the need to

comprehend, isn't that right? Comprehension is beneath artists, I suppose. Politicians are above the law. Artists are above thinking. I'll tell you what, I need to understand. I need— I need to— Let me out, Oscar. Now. Now.

Vomit in bathroom.

Note to self:

> Get
>
> your
>
> shit
>
> together
>
> you
>
> silly
>
> cow.

JUNE 20 :

Find Ranger standing guard outside Oscar's classroom. He doesn't want Oscar distracted from finishing the CAD/CAM plans.

Ranger looks a bit off.

JUNE 30 :

Another visit. Ranger is adrift. Grooming habits slipping. Complexion a shade paler than natural, as far as natural applies to Ranger. Seems Luis the Fabricator is not returning his calls.

Oscar in great spirits. Scratching away at refinements to the final six expressions of his formula. Pig in shit.

Me (to Oscar): So this might be good, right? Maybe Luis is blowing you guys off. It's good, right?

Oscar: My guess is Luis is passively admitting he's useless when it comes to this level of magnificence. Did he really think he could fabricate—this? (Arm-wavy dance before the chalk-boards.)

We put on some Afro-Pop and boogie like assholes. Ranger enters to spoil the fun. We pretend to study Oscar's latest amendment.

Despite myself, I catch a problem and we go at the formula for a few hours. Leaving, pass Ranger restlessly asleep at his desk. Drooly and forlorn. Neglected twelve-year-old.

JULY 4 :

Delia is up early, still giddy after our not-so-bad night together. Wants me as token brown companion for her blue-blood father's polo shirt bar-b-q out on the Cape. But Ranger calls and (fuck) Luis has arrived.

Haul ass to the school. Thinking must snuggy up to this Luis. Talk sense into him.

By time I arrive, seriously skilled road crew is setting up for what looks like a Pink Floyd concert in the gym. Impressions:

1. Nothing happenstance about the gear or methodology, i.e., Luis either has a genuine plan or is brilliant con artist (and wouldn't that be a fitting comeuppance for Ranger);

2. Ranger is back to old self—sanguine, deliberate, restored to workaday shade of pale, facial hair lines definitive;

3. Oscar wide-eyed, twitchy re: resolute progress of Luis's operations;

4. One of the crew members is named (sigh) Amber. Amber is in constant motion. Amber, Amber, willowy Amber.

Grab six-pack and Oscar by the shirt tail. Sit him down on the bleachers to watch the Luis-machine click through its paces.

Me: So, you had no clue?

Oscar: What?

Me: That Luis knows his shit.

Oscar: (nods)

Me: Bullshit, you didn't know.

Oscar: Part of me knew.

Me: Ah. Maybe you should be listening to that part more.

Oscar: (shrugs, sips beer)

Me: You're going to talk to Luis, right? You're going to warn him.

Oscar: (shrugs, chugs)

Wait for crew break. Bring Luis a beer.

Me: Wow. Very impressive. (re: splendor of the construction effort)

Luis: You like? You like my ecto-structure, yes?

Me: (lean closer, breast/upper arm contact) I am impressed.

Luis: Is brilliant theorem, this Oscar has. I am very excited by this. And have very great excitement for Ranger. This will be his most amazing work.

Me: Oh yes, very exciting. And a fitting end to his career.

Luis: (head back) Oh, but no, he—

Me: I mean, yes, maybe—there's a chance he'll survive.

Huge laugh. Bear hug. Onions and cologne.

Return to bleachers.

>**Oscar:** You need slut lessons.
>**Me:** (chug)

JULY 5 :

At Luis's invitation, crawl out of bed at half past ungodly for breakfast. On arrival, aroma of Luis's cooking makes me ache for him as a wife.

Oscar has butchered his hair. Looks like POW. Grumbling about Luis—re: tearing hole in the fabric of reality, etc.

>**Me:** You're blaming Luis? So now you're projecting your own guilt onto Señior Luis, who let's face it is a) not responsible for this plan and b) not up to the task of maintaining quantum coherence during an observed event, anyway.
>**Oscar:** And you're obsessed with my feelings of guilt. What does that mean, Freud-wise? Is there a term for your condition?
>**Me:** Said the man-boy with the cry-for-help haircut.
>**Him:** It could have been worse. My ears survived.
>**Me:** I call my condition rational. At best, Luis is an illusionist. All this, which—I mean it's staggeringly impressive technology and, yes, his track record of accomplishing crazily impossible logistical tasks in the art world, well—I mean, all that but, it doesn't mean he can, you know—
>**Oscar:** Did you see his schematics?
>**Me:** —because this might all look like a spectacular success right up until the point where he blunders spectacularly.
>**Oscar:** Did you see his schematics?

We look at his schematics. Luis has 256 quantum cascade lasers. Luis has ways to apply virtual substrates to alternating physical states. Luis has maybe a 1:25 chance of pulling this off, making an existential meltdown substantially less certain than cataclysmic climate change or the permanent loss of legal abortions in American, but this is going down soon—here, with us as witnesses, with us as accomplices, with Ranger in the role of space monkey.

Luis is bubbly with self-congrats.

> **Me to Luis:** How is it possible that you got your hands on this amazing equipment?
> **Luis:** Funny, yes? You wouldn't believe what things Ranger gets by promising piece of free art that someday it might be worth enough to buy some villa at Lake Como.
> **Me:** This is actually getting less funny by the day. Can we—shit, I don't know, can we just review the risks?

Clearly wrong thing to say. Luis's beams. Luis somehow turned on by prospect of universal peril.

Bear hug. Multiple alternate kisses, cheeks, forehead, scalp.

> **Luis:** So fucking exciting, no? Oh, we will tear up things, no?

And he exits. Oscar and I lock in mutual stare, seeing locomotives approaching in one another's eyes. Paralyzed by realization nothing short of sabotage will stop these self-worshipers.

Also (and this is perhaps the funny part) gripped by uncontrollable desire to know if the insane plan will work. Did they feel this way at Los Alamos? Did the vibrations rattling their bones say to them, you've given humans—simpleminded humans—a means of ending the world. Did any of this come to mind as they watched with childish glee as the first mushroom cloud took shape?

JULY 6 :

Return to the apartment around 2 am to find Delia and her obsequi-
ous excuses for friends, Josh and Claire, stupendously trashed. Dead
soldiers stacked in pyramid. What's-the-matter-can't-you-take-it look
from Delia.

I can't. Exit. She dogs me to the first landing, blubbering. Contest of
escalating accusations and declining intelligence.

> **Delia:** (ultimately) And don't you come back, bitch.
> **Me:** It's my place, jerk face. (never could sling an insult) You
> fucking get out.
> **Delia:** Fuck that. Fuck you. You get out. Fuck you.
> **Me:** No, fuck you.

And so on.

Back at the school, all are in their cots. Ranger is alone in the gym,
sitting mid-floor on a rotating stool. A series of odd zig-zaggy sketches
surround him, fanned out across the floor.

Drag a folding chair over and intrude myself amidst drawings.

> **Me:** Look at me. Ranger, look at me. I'm not messing around. I
> need your full attention on the safety issue. Are you considering
> the safety issue?
> **Ranger:** You seem disturbed.
> **Me:** Oh?
> **Ranger:** You're exhibiting signs.
> **Me:** You have to tell me what you're thinking. Are you thinking
> you're going to survive this project? Are you suicidal? I need to
> understand.

Ranger: (looks at my feet on his drawings) The most compelling dynamic of the performance is my unwillingness to let danger be a deterrent.

Me: OK, OK, see, right there, if you asked someone to define irresponsible behavior they would—

Ranger: It's well accepted behavior. In many professions, you can't succeed without it. A race car driver could not perform to the level required were he thinking about the risk of crashing, and that risk is considerable.

Me: I would argue he—or she—has a fuller understanding of the risks and how to avoid them. Do you understand what could happen to you? Are you taking precautions? Are you giving us the time and resources to take precautions?

Ranger: When the array goes on, I want to experience the moment with clear eyes, unclouded by trepidation. That will make me fully responsible, not irresponsible. It's my responsibility as an artist.

Me: What about the your responsibility to maybe not fuck up the universe?

Ranger: (looks at my feet again) I'd prefer you not step on my drawings.

Me: (move my chair back) What do these drawings mean, anyway?

Ranger: Why would you assume a drawing means something? Does a loaf of bread mean something?

Me: I'll have to consider that. Are these people?

Ranger: Yes, in a figurative sense.

Me: I guess I'm surprised you think that much about people, figuratively or otherwise.

Ranger: That was meant to be insulting. Sketching figures is a grounding exercise for artists. (staring at the laser array framework) People will always be people. But there's a broader consideration. As things go, what we've done here has not been hard to accomplish. Certainly, a full scale, well funded physical science facility could do something similar without much trouble, relative to, say, building a supercollider to smash protons together.

Me: Protons into anti-protons.

Ranger: As you say. And so, let me ask you, how long before someone else gets around to doing this? Is there some reason we shouldn't be the ones to do it? Is it better left to someone else?

Me: You're asking if it's better that someone else fucks up the universe? Are you being serious?

Ranger: (pause) Yes.

Me: There are protocols and safety procedures that would delay an experiment at an authorized lab by decades.

Ranger: In China? In Russia? In Iran, Israel, North Korea?

Me: We could work to ensure safeguards against its use.

Ranger: We would fail. At most perhaps we'd hold progress at bay during our lifetimes, but ultimately we would fail. Do you want to waste your life on a failed effort?

Me: We could swear to silence. Maybe Oscar's formula will never be discovered. Maybe this was a singular convergence of minds and circumstances that will never be repeated.

Ranger: You are I'm sure familiar with the theory that all advanced civilizations reach a point when they develop technology that presents an existential threat to their species. Humans have already learned to split the atom and have since come within a hair's breadth of worldwide nuclear holocaust. After decades, they seem to have learned nothing about diffusing the risk. Given the billions of possible planets where civilizations as foolish as ours, and possibly much more technically advanced than ours, might develop, and given the great expanse of time in which that might occur, a cataclysmic event that threatens the universe is virtually assured. You've heard this theory?

Me: (pause) Yes.

Ranger: And so it follows that even if we don't, some other civilization will undoubtedly develop a working model of Oscar's theorem. Perhaps one already has. Perhaps it's sitting in a desk drawer somewhere—here or out there somewhere—waiting to fall into the wrong hands—or claws or tendrils, as the case may be. And yet it's also likely, since all this foundational science we're using is at hand presently in our world, some other human physicist will build an array like this rather soon, probably within the next ten to twenty years. Am I wrong?

Me: But it's us, Ranger. It's not some theoretical other scientist or squid in a far galaxy in the future. It's us. Here. We need to—

Ranger: Am I wrong?

Me: You're stretching the logic to suit your whims. We have a responsibility to—

Ranger: I've addressed the responsibility question. As an artist, my responsibility it to my art. As a scientist, you're not responsible for avoiding risk to a universe that is already doomed.

I stand. I circle the array and come back to him.

He looks up from his drawing. Shake my head. Leave.

Wake up Oscar in his classroom. Tangled in his sheets, like Gandhi with bad hair.

Oscar: What? What's with you?

Me: I'm disturbed.

He reaches under the mattress for a joint.

Oscar: Girl trouble? (tokes)

Me: With us at the center of a devastatingly irresponsible plot to end the universe, why would you assume it's my pathetic relationship with Delia that is upsetting me?

Oscar: Plot? That's dramatic. It's an experiment. No, it's a work of art. No, it's an experiment. Oh, damn it, I just don't know anymore. You'll have to decide for the two of us.

Recount my conversation with Ranger.

Oscar: (tokes) Ranger sees the death of the universe by unnatural causes as inevitable. Makes sense. He figures, if so, it's worth risking an existential threat if great art comes from it. Why the fuck not? What doesn't make sense is his art—not to me, anyway. I guess I'm not as smart as patrons of the arts. Or maybe making no sense is essential to great art—I mean true art, not like Rembrandt and Monet and Van Gogh and such who made that superfluous shit that illuminates the beauty in the world.

Me: How conceited we are. Delia says she won't bring children into the world because it's so messed up. Who is she to decide for future children whether they want to live in this world? Do we think we understand enough about what the universe is thinking to make a call like this?

Oscar: The universe isn't thinking, not yet. (giggles)

Me: What?

Oscar: Have I told you about Micky's theory? Micky figures the universe is using humanity as an instrument to gain consciousness.

I take the joint and Bogart it down to a nub.

Me: (some time later) Say that again.

Oscar: All of creation, the evolution of life, etc. is all a grand design—wait, I can't use design. Christians use that word. And the universe isn't acting. There can't be will if there's no consciousness yet. Let's just say humanity is evolving into a sensory and cognitive instrument through which the universe may become conscious.

Me: OK, I can see that. People are really just devices that carry gene evolution forward. That's really been our only function as living organisms—self-perpetuation. But Micky's theory would suggest a higher purpose—universal consciousness.

O: Micky, bless his big murderous soul, he only saw the rosy side of that. Cosmic consciousness, bliss, rapture, blah dee blah blah. What if consciousness is not the endgame? What if the universal imperative is its own destruction? What if the universe is using us to find a way to end it all?

Me: And as instruments, we have no choice.

O: It's in our nature. We can't not. It's like seeing how far you can stick a Q-Tip in.

Me: The universe needs us for assisted suicide?

Oscar: Basically, and Ranger thinks that if we don't assist, somebody else will. Ranger and Micky—like two peas in a bipolar pod. I'm so blessed in my friendships.

Me: Ranger's your friend?

O: Did you ever hear the expression, foolishness is your friend?

Me: That's not an expression. Do you think of me like a sister?

O: I've never had a sister. Do you think your brother thinks of you like I do?

Me: I prefer not to consider that.

O: (sometime later) No. My answer is no. If I had a sister, I would feel weird thinking of her like I think of you.

Me: Would you like to demonstrate your feelings for me?

O: (sometime later) I am. This—here—is how I feel about you. Do you think I let other people wake me and ask me about helping the universe die? If we were more, well, demonstrable, this—here—would change in a probably unsatisfactory way. I've had a number of unsatisfactory relationships already, this year alone.

Me: Look at you, the mature one. OK.

O: OK, as in let's not? Because, if you—

Me: Let's not. I'm leaving in a little bit and I'm not coming back.

O: What? Why?

Me: Because you're right. This is going to happen. We're beyond the theoretical part that I can help with. From this point forward, I could only contribute to stopping it. And you want it to happen.

O: Sad, but true.

We nod off.

JULY 7 :

Wake with the dawn.

Find Amber outside smoking. She looks sleepy and ruffled.

She looks amazing.

> **Amber:** You going to the diner for coffee?
> **Me:** Am now.

We sit at the counter. The caffeine hits her with swift ferocity. As it happens, she's a light fiber sculptor. She's a poet. She works with words in light. She's an activist, but isn't active, and she thinks she's an anarchist, but maybe she's just an agitator. She used to want to be a pilot. She still wants to be a pilot. She isn't interested in the project per se, but loves lasers.

> **Me:** This project, it should bother you. You should leave.
> **Her:** Lasers are the purest sculptural medium, and I love the science pretense. I want to learn more about science stuff to build more pretension into my sculpture. And Luis doesn't hit on me, so it's chill. So, I'd rather not leave, for a few reasons like that. Why? What's going to happen?
> **Me:** We don't know. And what we don't know is unfathomably dangerous. And we might not know afterward either.
> **Amber:** I don't get it.
> **Me:** Look, I can't watch this train wreck, so I'm not going back there. You come and see me if you want, if things get scary. But the thing is, it may not get scary until it's too late. So, if I were you, I'd head back to Brooklyn.
> **Amber:** I can't, for a few reasons, like I said.

JULY 9 – AUGUST 11 :

Busy myself with fall lesson plans. Nothing from Oscar. Nothing from Ranger. Nothing from Delia. Nothing from Amber.

My usefulness it appears is at an end for all concerned.

AUGUST 12 :

New encounter with Amber, quite lovely.

Appears at my door bearing Rioja and molded soft cheese item.

We talk about her.

For four hours.

Works beautifully. Things progress.

> **Me:** (after, in bed) I don't want to ask you about what's going on there—there at the place.
> **Amber:** It's kinda crazy. It's actually very crazy what's about to— Well, you don't want to talk about it.
> **Me:** No, I wouldn't want to—
> **Amber:** It's all assembled. They're testing the—Sorry.
> **Me:** Array?
> **Amber:** It's just that I had no any idea what to expect.
> **Me:** So the tests have been successful?
> **Amber:** They're making a lot of adjustments—endless, endless adjustments. Must be three weeks now of fucking adjustments.
> **Me:** But it's rendering the impossible object?
> **Amber:** Yeah. I mean, shit, yeah. It's shit-crazy the way it—
> **Me:** Is the liquor store still open?

AUGUST 29:

Just before 11 pm, Amber on the phone, sounding distant. It's like I'm talking to the ten percent that's hovering above an anxiety attack.

Amber: Why didn't you tell me? Did Ranger tell you? Do you think Ranger is planning to get inside?"

Me: Well, yes. You didn't know?

Amber: Oh God, I knew it. This is not the least bit cool. I want to leave. I just want to get away from this.

Me: You should. You should come here. Do you need me to get you?

Amber: They're doing it tomorrow morning, Lakki. They're doing it for real. I don't think I can leave.

Me: You have to. I'll come get you.

Amber: No, don't. I don't think— Shit, I have to go. I have to go.

Pull jeans on over my PJs. Drive to within a few blocks. Stop.

Thinking: You idiot, you got the hell out. Stay smart. Stay away. Keep being smart.

More thinking: Amber and Oscar and Ranger and Luis and then there's Mumsy and Raj and Shikha and her little ones and tomorrow could be indescribably horrible for all of everything. This needs to be stopped. You can stop this.

More thinking: You can't stop this. Further, you won't be able to leave. No way you'd be able to not see it through. Be smart. Be smart, you ditsy cow.

Very rough K-turn. Head to McG's.

Two vodka gimlets along, sincerely sinister hottie slides onto the next stool. I motion to the bartender for a third.

Hottie: Yeah, that is you. You're Oscar's smart little bitch.

Steely eyes. Brows like slash-marks.

Me: I am smart. I am a very, very smart girl, which is why I'm here and not—well, wherever. But I am no one's bitch. Well, everybody's somebody's bitch, but I'm certainly not Oscar's bitch. Why? I mean, what's it to you?

Her: Oh, yeah, it's you. You and him at that freakin' high school doing whatever wicked weird shit, probably building bombs and what the hell. You fuckin' him?

Me: OK, so who are you again?

Crooked smile. Downs my shot.

Hottie: Haven't seen Oscar since I hole-punched his fuckin' shoulder. Bitch, I gotta tell ya, that felt nice. Ever stick an ice pick through a guy?

Me: Oh shit. You're—wait. Felicity?

Phoenicia: Phoe-ni-ci-a. So you two still working at that school on all that evil shit?

Me: Oh no, I'm gone. He is. And evil is wholly inadequate.

Motion for two more.

Ph: Evil is wholly inadequate—listen to you. Evil little prick, that Oscar. I don't mean bad. I'm bad. Micky knows how to be bad, but good. Micky has a good heart. He opened it up to that little prick and that was Micky's last mistake—last and worst in a long line of bad fuckin' mistakes.

Me: You were in that line too, from what I gather. From what I gather, it took both you and Oscar to cheat on Micky.

Ph: Well, you know what? You don't fuckin' understand. What I did to Micky was between me and him, something that me and him understood. Oscar, he should have never have took advantage of Micky like he did. Micky was all taken with Oscar—fuckin' genius Oscar with the fuckin' smart mouth. Oscar's just a little prick who had no business taking advantage of Micky's good heart.

Slide one of the drinks her way. We down.

Me: Maybe. Maybe you're right about Oscar.

Ph: Damn right, I'm right. I'm usually damn right, and Oscar's a little prick. So what about you? What's he doing at that place, anyway?

Me: Hard to explain.

Ph: Really, now. Ain't that just like you people. I understand more than you think, smart bitch. I saw the formulas on the board. I can see he's up to no good.

Me: Impressive. No, I just need a good way to explain. Let me think. What's your favorite sport?

Ph: Baseball.

Me: Oh. Second favorite?

Ph: Bowling.

Me: Brilliant. Imagine you're bowling. You're standing at the head of your bowling lane. You're preparing to bowl your bowling ball, and though you're completely unaware, to your left and right, are other Phoe-ni-ci-a's poised to bowl as well.

Remember thinking how massively clever this analogy is. Remember Phoenie nodding a lot as she dug through my pocket to buy us more drinks. Recall interruption from Big Jock Asshole with orange ski jacket. Recall Phoenie in short order reducing said BJA to tears. Recall celebrating her victory with Jägermeister. Recall handing her my keys. Arm-in-arm to my car.

AUGUST 30 :

In my back seat, askew against the door. Searing neck pain. Moist breath down below.

Phoenie's face is between my thighs, her right ear snuggled in my vagina like she's listening for ocean sounds. Her pants in a tangle around one ankle. Mine not present.

I so want to cry.

> **Me:** (aloud, I think) I just opened my eyes on my last day.
> **Phoenie:** (throat gurgle)

Thighs feel sloppy. Phoenie's drool.

Onset of headache like only one responsible for end of world deserves. Horrific urge to pee.

Alternating waves—remorse, self-loathing.

Impenetrably

dark

blanket

of

dread

Phoenie gurgles. Emits moist sputters of effluvia, then convulses from diaphragm. I snatch at door handle and lurch sideways as she vomits.

Standing half naked in the school parking lot, hugging the roof, face on metal, hot from the morning sun.

Crying/peeing uncontrollably.

Time elapses (indeterminate).

> **Oscar:** Hi. As befits the situation, in a moment I'm going to let you know that everything is going to be OK.
> **Me:** It's our last day, Oscar.
> **Oscar:** I can imagine there are circumstances when that might come off as touching and sad.
> **Me:** I'm so sad. I'm so sad.
> **Oscar:** Lakshmi?
> **Me:** What?
> **Oscar:** Everything is going to be OK.

Peals me from side of car and wraps gym towel around my waist. Turn to see a gaggle of important somebodies of some sort making their way into the school. They turn to avoid staring. Classy bunch.

(involuntary belch)

> **Me:** (in Oscar's ear) Is there a drug that will help me get through whatever this is?
> **Oscar:** What kind of stupid question is that? Of course.
> **Me:** I'm sorry. I'm so sorry. (indeterminate repetitions)
> **O:** Please shut up. I really don't want Phoenie to wake up.

Oscar makes pit stop at his stash on way to locker room. Doses me: 2 mg of Xanax; 20 mg of Ritalin. Escorts me to showers.

Fifteen minutes later, wonder at life-sustaining marvel that is hot water. Perhaps the universe is worth one final effort.

Ultra-low frequency hum cycle, blooming/receding. Sending seismic shimmies through puddles on the shower stall floor.

Oscar waiting for me on a bench with borrowed sweats. Fills me in as I dress.

Yes, all systems go. Yes, the press, art luminaries, money people of no worth save their money are in attendance, sequestered in the old teachers' lounge with 30 sec delay video feed. Ranger presently recording a statement for the press, to be released publicly in the ostensible post-event future.

Me: Is Amber OK?

Oscar: Haven't seen her. She was AWOL at the system check.

Me: And what about Ranger? Is he keeping it together?

O: Sure, sure.

Me: Dumb question. Must be basking in radiant visions of his own impending martyrdom.

O: Wow, I like how this drug cocktail sounds on you. You're almost—

No, that wouldn't be nice.

Me: What?

O: I was going to say poetic. Sorry.

Me: That's OK.

O: But I'm not sure that explains Ranger, the martyr complex. My theory about Ranger is— Never mind. It's just too late to get into this.

Me: Seriously? What?

O: Are you going to stay and help me? (stands) Let's go in.

Me: What theory? What about Ranger?

O: (Sits) I think he knows he's going to make it through.

Me: Knows as in harbors an unfounded belief or knows knows? What could he know we don't know?

O: Knows as in this isn't his first time. He's survived before, or I should say, he's surviving it many times—now. Oh, fuck it.

Me: Why would you think that?

Tells me how Ranger let it slip at McG's one night soon after the accident that he was present in the van.

Oscar: And again, that night we did the 'shrooms, he said I died.

Me: You died? In your van accident? Wow. How do you feel about that?

O: Hard to process without the right drugs. But the point is, he seems to know stuff that he shouldn't know.

I'm buzzed in a sort of aggressively mellow way. Dark honey and rose patches of loveliness swarming about my peripherals. I dub them Amber-Glows in my mind.

Straddle bench and face Oscar. Put hands on his thighs.

Me: Look at me.

O: Kind of hard not to when you're—

Me: Are you thinking what I'm thinking?

O: Well yeah, I just clued you in. Remember, that was me who just told you about how Ranger—

Me: You go. You say it first.

O: OK. Ranger is experiencing—

Me: —multiple episodic states.

O: I was going to say multiverse fragmentation. I might like yours better.

Me: You died. Like another time, you died in the accident. And

Ranger, or the Ranger that was in that time, was with you. Did he die too?

O: Not another time. Same time. Other versions of the same time. Same me. Same Ranger. There's only one time and there's only one me and one him.

Me: But you don't remember any of the other versions?

O: No, nothing. And somewhat grateful not to remember being incinerated in the crash.

Me: You think Ranger is able to remember? All of the episodes?

O: That's my Ranger theory. What's most puzzling is why this is happening to him before he's been subjected to the array. I'm thinking different versions of Ranger are able to collaborate. They're forming a sort of common memory.

Me: That's nuts. How could he keep his shit together with all that happening in his brain—all those memories folded in together?

O: Ranger, the man who sits for days on end doing apparently nothing? Maybe he's trying to cope. Maybe he's processing.

Me: But he's, you know—weird.

O: Truly, and likely from birth. And as he says, his whole weird life as an artist prepared him for this.

Me: We thought he was a pretentious, preening, self-obsessed jerk. So embarrassing to learn he's been preparing to play hop-scotch back and forth across the multiverse.

Massive clunk. Relays engage and rattle the lockers. Echoes roll down the hallway.

Oscar: Come on. We'll have a few minutes to talk to him.

Pass Ty and Parker as we enter the gym, consumed in their clipboards. I ask about Amber. The generator drone now overwhelming.

Ty: (shouts) Gone. Halfway to Brooklyn by now.

Ranger enthroned on his twirly stool at the gym's midpoint. Hooded terrycloth gown. Doing utmost to block out Luis, who's on a ladder making an adjustment, shouting out everything he's thinking.

Luis: One more. Ah, y aquí. Si, good, good. All good—I can just
I think get this. Yes, good. Ah, Lakshmi is returned. Muy bien.
You are here, no, for the— Do you call it histrionics?
Me: One might, yes.

Luis stows ladder away. Embraces Ranger. Shouts unwanted encouragement in his ear. Administers likely unwanted neck rubbing.

Luis: Lakshmi, dearest—you must exit with me—ahora.
Lakshmi, now. Only these two will be present, say these
scientists.
Me: I'm one of these scientists, and I need a word with His
Highness. I'll be along.

Shakes head. Points to ears. Points to the ceiling. Lights flicker as if on command. Noises cascading. Broad spectrum of harmonic colors building to immense volume.

Intercom: (barks) Three minutes. Three minutes.
Me: Go, Luis. Go. Get—the—fuck—out—Luis.

Bulges eyes. Smiles. Shrugs. Exits.

Join Oscar, kneeling at Ranger's white feet. Assume he's trying to talk sanity into Ranger. Should have known. They're talking about Oscar.

Ranger: Your death was inescapable, Oscar. The accident was unstoppable. And there was simply no way to explain what I was experiencing there in the van.

Oscar: Well, actually, I'm a theoretical physicist, so, in theory, I might have understood.

R: Noted, as you voiced to me innumerable times in modestly different ways in the back of your van. But the fact that you might have understood wouldn't have helped me describe the inexplicable to you, especially in your incapacitated state. I tried to do so, innumerable times in modestly different ways.

Oscar to Me: See, he admits it.

Me to Ranger: But how can that be? You haven't been under the array yet.

R: Not in this version. Things occurred earlier in others.

Me: How in hell are you handling it? Tell us what you're feeling.

R: As previously, impossible to describe.

Me: Impossible? For Ranger? Isn't it your role as an artist to explain the inexplicable?

R: That's a pedestrian interpretation.

Me: (wait him out)

R: (unblinking unblinking) I'm sitting in on a recording session. I'm in the recording booth. The musicians lay down dozens of tracks, and dozens of takes of each track. I don't have headphones, so I can't hear until, at a point, the producer lends me his set and I hear a single take—a single take of one instrument. I hand the headphones back and observe as the producer records take after take. I have no sense which takes he is choosing. I can't hear his mix, so I have no sense of the layered whole. In my head is just the memory of one isolated take. The producer hears the complete mix that coalesces into a song.

Oscar: OK, so you're now the producer. You're hearing all the parts, all the possibilities of how each moment is played, as each moment is happening.

R: Yes.

O: But are they coalescing?

Me: Are you hearing a melody?

R: (unblinking unblinking.) I'm learning. I'm trying.

O: You're going to be OK then? We're going to survive? Wait. (pulls Ranger's hood back) What the fuck did you do?

Ranger's head is clean-shaven, scalp, face.

Ranger: (stands, disrobes) I've depilated.

Me: Wow. So white.

Oscar: Why would you do that?

Me: White. I'm blind.

R: I believe, it may make a difference. It was an intuitive decision.

O: Difference to what? Why?

Ranger steps past us toward the containment structure.

Intercom: Thirty seconds. Thirty seconds.

R: Don't read too much into it.

O: Hair? You're planting this in my head at this moment?

Ranger continues forward. Unzips the containment tent.

Oscar takes my arm.

O: We have to leave. Both of us.

Me: What? No, you're going to stay and observe, right? If you're not then I'm—

Oscar tugs at his hair. Tugs on my hair.

Me: Seriously? You're taking the hair thing seriously?

Ranger is entering the array. Inter-folding translucencies as the lasers intersect his form.

Oscar has me from behind, arms around my waist. Pulls me out into the hallway.

We run to the teacher's lounge. It's packed to the door with the rich and superfluous. Oscar forges a path to monitors using a gray-templed somebody as a plow.

Generator hum louder here. Multiple camera views. In one, with the delay, Ranger has just entered the array. From another, me and Oscar arguing with our hands. Oscar spins me, tries to get me around the waist. I stiff-arm him, put him off balance. He trips and hits the floor. I help him up. We exit.

I make sure he's seeing what I'm seeing.

Oscar: OK, that did not happen. You didn't knock me down.
Me: Apparently I did.

Room chatter rises. One camera is tight on Ranger's face, calm as a lake. Lasers inter-cutting, images rippling, splitting, reassembling.

Ranger's eyes are steady. He's saying something. Repeating something. A short phrase.

Some too-skinny woman in black suit: (shouting) What's he saying?

Older woman in black, also skinny, drastically asymmetric hair: (shouting) Who can read lips?
Amber: (yes, Amber is present) He's saying, I am—
Too-skinny woman #1: I am the one—the one—
Oscar: I am a walrus.

Image goes blocky, then white, then blocky.

Room hushes. Generator clacks, then resolves to hollow whine.

Oscar beckons for Ty. He comes to the control board and punches up another camera. No good. Then another. Zooms in on Ranger's face.

Room erupts with shouting.

> **Too-skinny woman #1:** He's saying I am unnerved. No, I am invaded. I am envied.
> **Ty:** Yes, that's it! I am invaded.
> **Asymmetric-old-skinny:** I am alive.
> **Amber:** No, no, no! Shut up. He's saying, I am your voice.
> **General agreement:** Yes, it's definitely I am your voice. So poignant. Polemic!

Oscar is shaking head.

> **Me:** I know.

Video degrades into in various configurations of blockiness. Then generator chunks hard. Then again. Then begins its wind-down. Hum cycles down, octave by octave. Gentle whir.

> **Room:** (panting)

The monitors snap to sharp resolution. Ranger is on his way out of the array enclosure—30 seconds ago.

Oscar spins. I follow as he wedges through multiple women in black to the door.

> **Oscar to everyone:** All of you stay here. Everyone.

General protestations.

> **Oscar:** (leans back through door) Look, stay put. You want to fuck up this whole thing? Just stay the fuck put for ten minutes.

We run to gym—no Ranger. Run to Oscar's classroom, the bathrooms, the showers, then back to the classroom.

I sit. Oscar paces.

Oscar is smiling.

> **Me:** What?
>
> **Oscar:** You saw what he said.
>
> **Me:** I am the universe.
>
> **O:** And you saw what just happened, version-wise.
>
> **Me:** Happened is such an inadequate word.
>
> **O:** Shut the fuck up. What just happened?
>
> **Me:** We experienced something different in the gym than what the video feed picked up.
>
> **O:** Right. What else?
>
> **Me:** Amber never left. But she left. She was hours away when the array kicked on. But now, she never left.

Oscar laughs. Hard. Forehead down to knees hard.

> **Me:** And the other thing is, Ranger may have achieved universal consciousness.

Oscar snorts. Wipes his eyes.

> **O:** No, no, according to the Law of Micky, it's the other way around. The universe has achieved Ranger. I'm guessing Ranger planned a one-step-for-mankind moment with the I am the universe line. But maybe he was feeling something for real.

We sigh. Multiple sighs. He smiles again.

> **Me:** What?
>
> **O:** Did I tell you about my grandfather? I liked my grandfather.

Me: Good for you.

O: It's notable because I dislike everyone in my family, with the exception of Grandpa Ralph. Grandpa Ralph was OK.

Me: No, you never told me.

O: I used to eat dinner sometimes with Grandpa Ralph. He lived alone and I liked any excuse to not be home, so I'd go to his apartment. One night, after dinner—

Me: Oh, I see. This is an anecdote. So not you.

O: Correct. One night, we're doing the dishes. He's loading the dishwasher. Oh, I should preface this by saying this is why I began thinking about physics.

Me: OK. What did you think about before that?

O: Not relevant. So this one night, I'm scraping and washing. He's loading the dishwasher. He opens the dishwasher door— and, oh, I should also say that he was half loopy, Grandpa Ralph, which is another reason I went over there a lot because no one else fucking cared to look in on him and—

Me: Get back to the dishes.

O: Right. So he opens the dishwasher door and stands there staring at the silverware. The silverware tray is full of clean silverware. He forgot to unload the silverware earlier in the day when he unloaded the other stuff. He left the silverware—

Me: Please stop saying silverware.

O: Sorry. He has this, I don't know, delighted look on his face. He was delighted by the surprise that forgetting gave him. He says, Let me give you some advice, Oscar. He says, Oscar, just 'cause you forget stuff, doesn't mean it's not there.

Me: OK, so in this analogy, we're Grandpa Ralph?

O: The human race is Grandpa Ralph. Ranger is experiencing a bunch of possibilities of how moments occur, and he's remembering everything. Regular humans forget all but one possibility. We only remember we what need to know to get by. But all the other possibilities are there—well, possibly—potentially.

Me: But when we witnessed Ranger under the array, we got sucked along into another version of the event? And now we're remembering two possibilities. Is that what you're thinking?

O: I think we're— I think this is another version, now, here. And what's that noise?

Tapping, coming from the adjacent classroom.

Oscar: Somebody's writing on the blackboard next door.

Me: There is no blackboard next door. The room next door is stripped bare and always locked.

We turn the handle and enter. It's furnished, lived in. Racks of art supplies and rolls of paper, cafeteria tables used as drawing desks. Dozens of Ranger's cubist-y figurative sketches are posted. Scale models of the array fill much of the floorspace, complete with Ranger action figures in position.

The blackboard is covered in diagrams. Ranger is there (naked glory), drawing away. Turns to us as we enter. Resumes his work.

Oscar approaches him. Ranger's renderings depict the van incident. A prostrate figure coiled in cloth, like a mummy. In many, an oversized figure hovers above. Others document the accident scene from a bird's eye view. Others map out the course along city streets. Multiple routes. Dozens.

Oscar: You have hair again.

Ranger: (pauses his work) Go ahead. Ask.

Oscar: What? Ask what?

Ranger: (taps on his drawing) You have questions.

Oscar: (pause, then) Will events keep duplicating for me and Lakshmi?

R: Yes, you will probably open up to more of what's occurring in the other— What word should we use?

O: Versions.

R: Versions. (taps again) What do you really want to know?

O: Can you put on some pants?

R: (taps again)

Oscar: (stares. stares) Did I really try to kill Micky?

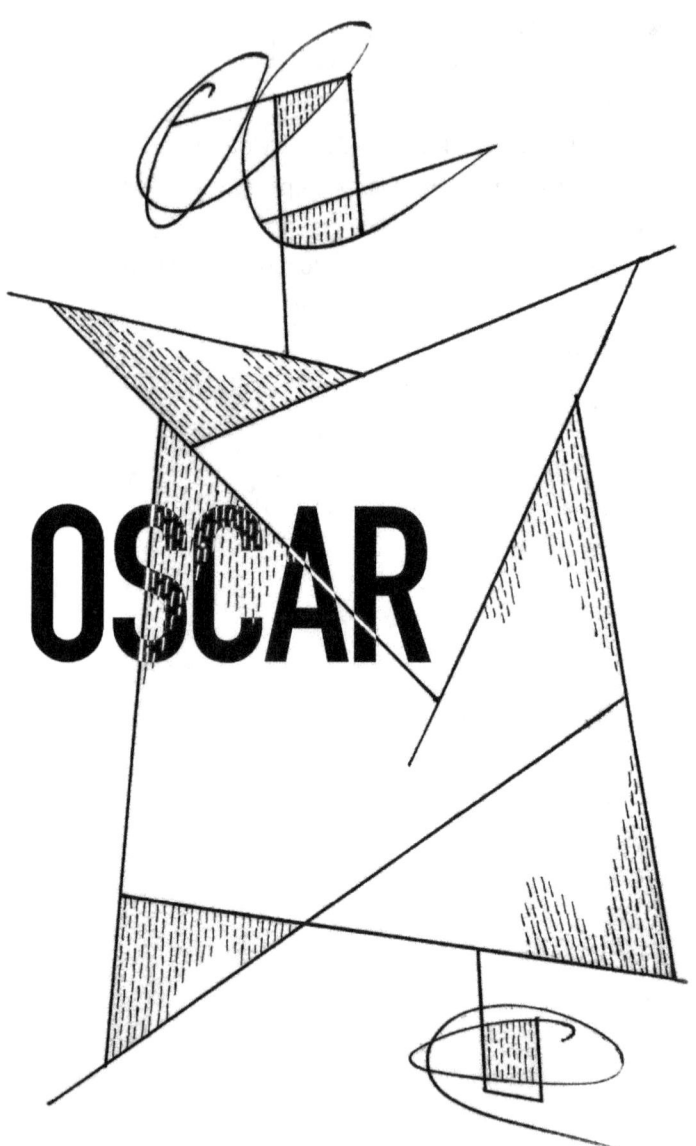

CHAPTER SEVEN

Following the impossible figure incident, Oscar is faced with the complication of living parallel lives.

Oscar turned right off the elevator onto the long hallway and passed rooms astir with chatty visitors.

Dining tray carts and bored kids littered the hall, but no cop was in sight. Oscar entered through the last door on the left and found a custodian cleaning an empty room. He stepped back out to check the room number—528.

"Did they move him?" Oscar said, leaning inside.

She shrugged without interrupting her mopping strokes.

He inquired at the nurses' station.

"No. We haven't had a Micky Green," said Nurse Stiegmire.

"It's Michael, actually. Try Michael."

She tapped the keyboard some more. "Michael Resnick Green. Rehabilitation."

"What? No. You sure it's—"

"—the same Michael Resnick Green? You'll know when you see him. Elevator to three."

Downstairs, Oscar worked his way through the geriatric ward to a wide common rehab area. A dozen or so beds lined the periphery, most cordoned off with privacy curtains. In the center of the room, a physical therapist knelt on a mat and bent a patient's leg toward her chest. Another therapist circled round in a wheelchair, offering encouragement.

Oscar asked them about Micky.

"Hey, hey, Oscar, that you?"

Oscar turned and parted the curtains behind him. Micky sat cross-legged against a pile of pillows at the head of his bed, thighs bouncing. His left arm was in a sling. Tape and gauze covered his left ear. Above it, he was missing a broad swath of hair.

Micky stretched his good arm wide. "Come here. No hug? Haven't seen you in a dog's ass."

"Micky. What? Look at you. Wait, I don't get—"

"Look at me? What's with what your face is doing, man?"

"Bring refreshments this time, you cheap dick?"—this from a second voice. Oscar stepped inside and saw to his right a visitor sitting near the foot of the bed. His scalp was buzzed and creased with a brutal scar spanning the left temple.

"Tookie?" said Oscar. "Tookie— Tookie you..."

Oscar's shoulder hit the bed as he collapsed. He rebounded into the curtain and slid to the floor.

Micky guffawed. "Dig Oscar with the dramatic entrance."

Tookie stretched out a leg and nudged Oscar a few times until he came around.

Oscar sat up and clutched his ankles for stability. He looked at Tookie and then lowered his head between his knees.

Micky laughed on. "Must be working you half dead at that labor -atorium, Oscar. They allocate all the food to the test bunnies? And how are the bunnies? Funny? They feed you breakfast today? I know artists aren't keen on eating. That freak artist trying to starve you into obedience? I can tell you from my dog experiences that that just gets 'em mean. But you don't seem mean. You seem befuddlesome. How 'bout you, Took? You get regular feedings at home these days, right? Your new Scummie girl-squeeze been cooking it up? Get breakfast today?"

"Breakfast of Champions," said Tookie.

"Damn, I knew it. Pussy!" Micky shouted. "Oh, I will soon be fully restored to health, comrades. I am soon pussy-bound!"

"Hey, chill, yo!" called the physical therapist from outside.

"Fuck you, Jamal," Micky said. "Come here, Jamal. I don't think you measured my penis yet today. Remember how it grew last time you measured it?"

"OK now, Micky," said Jamal. "Just chill. People need some peace from you. Enough from you today already."

Tookie reached into the grocery bag beside him. He pulled out a folded newspaper and slapped it down beside Oscar. "Here ya go, hot shot. Local dope fiend enters the big leagues."

Oscar opened the paper to a three-column photo, a group shot with Ranger standing at center in his terrycloth robe. Ranger was flanked on the left by Luis and crew. Amber was half out of frame on the end. On Ranger's right stood an elegant silver haired woman in black, looking haughty, and Oscar, hands in pockets, looking shell-shocked.

The headline read, "No Charges Yet Filed, Agencies Wrestle Over 'Impossible Figure' Jurisdiction."

Tookie dragged his chair over and helped Oscar up, then circled to another seat on the far side of the bed.

Oscar followed Tookie's movements, nodding and blinking.

Tookie raised his eyebrows at him. "OK, what's with you, pilgrim?"

Oscar rubbed his face. He looked down at the newspaper. "Can't explain. Can't."

"Not to bitch," said Micky, "and not to further disturb your delicate sensibilities, but what was the very last thing I said to you, Oscar boy, last time you were here?"

Oscar looked at him. His eyes went moist. "You said, nothing is sacred. You said there is no truth."

Micky piffed. "That sound like me?"

"Yes?" said Oscar.

"Bring me a sausage calzone from Roma's or you're not welcome, were my precise words."

"Oh," said Oscar. His eyes drifted toward Tookie, then back again. "I can leave."

"Whoa. OK, you're worrying me, man," Micky said. "You all ker-flumpt about the legal turmoil, that it? That's Grade A bullshit, seems to me. Fucking visionary like you goes and takes a quantum leap of imagination and the scientific folks go all tribal with jealousy, am I right? Now they're itching to throw you to the legal wolves—the slope-brained sub-species of bastard lawyers drooling over new lucrative lawsuits they can feed on for decades. I mean, post-experiment, you and the crew, you're all functional, right?"

Oscar nodded.

"You're not peeing around corners, are you?" said Micky. "You're still breathing out after you breathe in and not the other way round? And we the general species, we're all still functionally illiterate as usual, right? What's changed? Where's their case, man?"

Oscar refolded the newspaper and laid it on the bed. "Yes, bullshit. Nobody got hurt, or at least not in a way they'll recognize."

"Absolutely." He cleared his throat. "Recognize what?"

"Nothing. Can't explain."

"Is it the whacko artist moon-bat? He get damaged? His atomics get scrambled? How about you, neurons get disco-bob-o-lated? Is that what's up with you? Got quantum disco-ball-brain? And where is the Loonie Ranger anyway? They say he splee-daddled."

"Ranger rhymes with hangar," said Oscar. "Don't know. He owns a few houses. Maybe Chile. Maybe Thailand."

"Ha. Left you doin' the 'splaining," said Tookie. "Slick artist fuck."

Oscar looked back at Tookie. He started blinking again. His mouth drifted open, then his face crimped. He drifted into snotty sobs.

Micky and Tookie waited him out, waving off Jamal when he peeked in to see who might need assistance.

"Sorry," Oscar said, after some time. "Been happening, since the experiment."

"Not a mystery, brother. You contracted post-stress. Clearly, you got it from the experiment you did on Arteest Le Freak. So, please explain, Oscar boy. Inquiring friends—your only true friends—want to know what went the fuck down. What was the nature of the trauma?"

"Bug got stuck in the gizmo, I bet," said Tookie. "Ranger Hangar got turned into a giant something or other and tried to suck your guts out."

"Hey, have some empathy, Took," said Micky. "The man's been presumably and possibly irreparably traumatized in some quantum fashion. Oscar is a young laddie of delicate sentiment. Unlike others present, he's got self-empathetical feelings. Oscar is not the particular kind of brute what can get whacked upside the head with a tire iron and let bygones be bygones."

"You might be overestimating my forgiveness," said Tookie.

"Noted," said Micky. "That's not to imply I'm not grateful, Took, for your forbearance, and in particular for not pressing charges. You're a righteous citizen, Took. Micky loves you for that. Micky thanks you. Micky's future generations of delinquent youths thank you, for being that I've been cooped up here for weeks, I will soon undoubtedly disseminate my seed liberally amongst the female populace forthwith and generate spawn. Had I been incarcerated, said youths might never have graced the sidewalks of our fair burg given the difficult, though not impossible, challenge of disseminating from behind and through prison bars."

"Not a problem," said Tookie. "And your dad, he's gonna have Oscar's van all beat back into shape before next week so I can make Dark Metal Fest up in Hampshire, right, with the addition of new sub-woofers and mags, right?"

"As was the condition," said Micky.

"Gratitude noted. No problem. No charges filed." said Tookie. "Also noted is Oscar's deep in that he's endowing me with his wheels, given I took one in the fucking skull for him, me being the stand-up guy in this group versus one anger management poster boy and one low life ex-Scummer who stooped to the act which shall forever never again be spoken of—you know, doing Phoenie."

Oscar stared at the floor, gripping his kneecaps to quell the shakes. He cleared his throat. The guys fell quiet.

"Here's the thing," said Oscar, closing his eyes. "Last time I came by, Micky, you were under house guard—shackled. Third degree over ninety percent."

Oscar's throat went raspy. He took a moment to slow his breath, then went on.

"You were shackled to the bed. And you said that shit. Nothing's sacred. There's no truth. Tookie, you were dead—back of the van, last I saw you. Your dead body. You, Micky, you got behind the wheel. You took off. Pretty sure I tried to kill you with the tire iron. I've only got fragments. You driving the van like a crazed bitch, crazy with remorse, crazy suicidal. Me stabbing you with the tire iron. The van hitting something, flipping. Fucking fireball. I got thrown out the back, they say. Hardly a scratch. You got burned to fuck—third degree over ninety percent."

"Wait, so—" Tookie looked at the ceiling. "So, you're saying I was—"

"You didn't make it. Micky killed you, on the street. He probably would've killed himself and me along for the ride. I tried to stop him."

"But—" Tookie was stroking his scar.

"He stoved your head in, Took. Threw you in the back of the van. You were dead, man. Micky, you got burned to shit. You are— You are burned to shit. Better off dead. I came here today figuring you'd be damn close to dead. And Took, you are dead. Like now. Dead."

They sat for a few moments. Then Tookie stood and pulled the curtain closed. He went into his grocery bag and handed out beers.

Once they were halfway through their first, Micky said, "What you just told us, that was no dream."

"No."

"All this you're saying, this is because of your experiment, right?"

Oscar nodded. "It's real. It's still really happening. This here—you doing fine, Tookie not dead—it's happening too, and that other version, happening too."

Micky blew out his cheeks. He adjusted his sling and stretched his neck. "OK, so now's when I should say this is all a figment of your post-trauma, right? So would it surprise you if everything you said sounded—I don't know, familiar? It's not like it's something I dreamed or daydreamed or wondered—never occurred to me. But the moment you said it—as you were saying it—I could remember it like I'd always remembered it."

"Déjà vu," said Tookie.

Micky pointed at him. He shook his finger. "Yeah, yeah. Total déjà vu. But much realer. You too?"

Tookie squinted. "No. I mean, kinda, but no. Like something's twinging at the side of my brain."

Micky wiped the back of his neck. "Damn, lizard sweat, man. It's like it happened—me laying in bed burned up. This isn't trauma, though, is it buddy? It's not post-stress from the accident and it's not post-stress from the experiment, 'cause why would I be feeling your post-stress? My friend, oh, you seriously fucked with something that shouldn'ta been fucked with."

They sat silent for a while.

"Actually," said Micky, "not true. Whatever you fucked with, we had it coming. It's human destiny. It's universal destiny. You know what I'm saying, don't you Oscar-boy?"

Oscar nodded. "Yeah, all that. So, there's this, though. Since the experiment, Ranger's been—well, what's happened to him is pretty much impossible to describe. And Lakshmi, she's bad like me, confusion-wise. And now that you're coming into contact—now that you're observing me—you're being mildly fucked with, which probably accounts for the déjà vu. But maybe you're both OK and should continue to be OK. Then again, could be not. Could be everything will change. Can't say yet."

Tookie grunted. "Great."

"That other me killed Took." said Micky. "That what you're saying?"

Oscar shook his head. "No, not another you. You, man. All you."

Micky and Tookie exchanged looks.

Oscar stood up, downed the rest of his can and set it on Micky's swing table. "And as for the universe, stop with the destiny bullshit. Nothing is destined to be. Anything could be anything a thousand ways to Sunday."

Oscar parted the curtains, but paused. "Oh, and Micky, remember your eyes-of-the-universe thing? Ranger, he might just be it—now. Maybe he's helping the universe be God."

"What?" said Micky. "What are you—"

"So, yeah," said Oscar. "But hard to say."

He turned and left.

Lakshmi exited the elevator and spun back to block the doors from closing. Oscar stood leaning against the back wall.

"Five, right?" she said.

"Yeah, 528." He pushed off and followed her.

The policeman glanced up from his paper as they approached.

"Family members only," he said.

"Lakshmi, this is Officer Brian," said Oscar. "We go way back."

"Ain't happening, not for you in particular." The officer turned his newspaper for them: "University Disavows Knowledge Of 'Impossible Figure' Experiment."

From the room came the hollow rasp of a ventilator and the familiar acrid smell.

"Let 'em in Murphy." The gravelly command came from inside.

"I dunno, Mr. Green. Highly questionable, particularly considering."

Oscar took Lakshmi's hand and walked in.

Otz Green sat at his son's bedside, leaning forward over his knees, his face colorless and unshaven. He motioned them to chairs.

Micky lay unconscious, breathing tube in place, the rise and fall of his chest barely perceptible beneath the sheets. A few bandages had been removed, revealing rusty scar tissue.

Oscar gave Otz a questioning look.

"Pneumonia," Otz said.

They sat without speaking for a while.

Lakshmi took a breath and stood. She offered Otz her hand. "I'm sorry, I'm Lakshmi. I'm sorry about Micky."

Otz's hand dwarfed hers. "Haven't heard your name."

"No. No, I didn't know him. I don't know him."

Otz nodded. He motioned to Oscar to close the door.

He turned to Micky for a moment as his son's breath stuttered. "What happened?" he asked Oscar.

Oscar rubbed the back of his neck. "Look, I was dead drunk—nearly dead."

Otz held up his palm. "Just tell me."

Oscar gave his account of the night of the accident, then told him another version, as best he could recall.

When he was done, Otz sat back. He stared at the door for a bit, then said, "Which is the real one?"

"Both," said Oscar. "I can't explain."

"Why the fuck not?"

Oscar stared back.

"It has to do with the experiment," Lakshmi said.

Otz cocked his head. "Your science had something to do with this here? With Micky?"

"No, it has to do with me," said Oscar, "with what I remember."

"Why would you hit him?" said Otz. "He was driving and you snuck up and hit him?"

"Probably. But like I said, there were two—"

Otz shook his head.

"I hit him to stop him from killing us—himself, me. That's what I remember."

"With a tire iron," said Otz.

"I was drunk, and I was frozen half to death, and I don't know what the hell I was thinking."

Otz patted his breast pocket and pulled out a nearly empty pack of cigarettes.

He stood. "Stay with him until I get back."

He stopped at the door. "I don't want him to be alone," he said.

"OK," said Oscar.

Lakshmi sat with Oscar. Much of the time, Oscar had his eyes closed. Occasionally he started, as if waking from a dream.

Lakshmi gazed out through the picture window for a while, the room's cold reflection layered over the evening cityscape. At times, she would giggle or groan or shake her head as if clearing unsound thoughts.

She volunteered to fetch some food and left without waiting for a response.

About forty minutes later, Micky's monitor alarm tripped. The beeping continued for five minutes. Oscar stuck his head outside.

"She's got higher priority patients," said Officer Brian, head resting against the wall.

Oscar fetched the nurse.

Nurse Lucia made an adjustment to the breathing apparatus and refreshed an IV.

"What's wrong? Did something happen?" Oscar asked her.

"Are you up on his condition?" she said.

"No."

"Sepsis. His kidneys are failing—liver too, probably."

She monitored him for a few more minutes, then turned and left.

Lakshmi returned with sandwiches about an hour thereafter.

"Sorry, that was a long time, wasn't it?"

"I think so," said Oscar.

"It's so easy to—you know, there."

Oscar nodded. "I'm downstairs."

"Now? Where downstairs?"

"I'm with Micky. He's in rehab."

"What?"

"He's much better—downstairs. And Tookie—" His voice broke.

"What?"

"Tookie didn't die. Tookie is downstairs in the room visiting. And Micky's going to be fine."

"Holy shit. That's great."

"Yeah."

"So, Micky didn't kill him? Tookie?"

"No. They're downstairs having a beer—with me."

She sat and turned to look out the window again.

Oscar took a sandwich. "How about you? Where are you?"

She smiled. "In the shower." She laughed. "I'm taking a very, very long shower."

"What are you thinking about, in the shower?" He handed her half a sandwich.

"About being here. About how this tuna melt smells. About telling you about the shower. I've just lathered myself up for the third time."

"That's good. Tell me what you're lathering exactly. This is helping me stay present."

"Fuck you."

They sat in silence, each breaking into laughter from time to time.

"This is so insane, Oscar. What are we going to do?"

He didn't reply.

"How are we going to live two lives, Oscar?" she said.

At eleven-thirty, he told her to go.

"Do you want me to try to find Otz?" Lakshmi said.

"How would you do that?"

"I don't know. I could—"

"No."

She stood a few moments watching Micky, then stepped close and picked up his hand. She turned it and stroked his palm.

"Are you still downstairs?" she asked Oscar.

"No. I'm heading over to your place with a bunch of freshmen girls."

She nodded. "Knock hard. I think I fell asleep listening to music."

She laid Micky's hand down, and left.

Lakshmi opened her door, headphones around her neck.

Oscar brushed past. "You're awake."

"Sounded like the door was going to give way."

She checked the hallway behind him, then followed him to the kitchen, kicking a sneaker into a corner and snatching a bra off a chair.

"Where's your harem of freshmen?" she said.

Oscar located her vodka and a clean glass. He cracked the contents of a plastic ice tray onto the counter, considered the state of the surface and poured his vodka straight.

"I know it sounds trivial given how screwed up everything is," said Lakshmi, leaning against the door frame, "but do me a favor and don't lie to me about what's happening with your counterpart?"

"My #2?"

"Yes. I'm confusing enough as it is without having to deal with your cutesy lying."

Oscar downed a shot and reached back for the bottle. "It wasn't a lie," he said. "I ran into a lovely young thing at the laundromat and she accompanied me most of the way here. And she had a notion to invite her roomies."

"Lovely, young and dense if she didn't recognize you from the papers —or did she, after all?"

He paused the glass by his lips. "She recalled a commitment to a previous engagement."

Oscar took a seat at the kitchen table. He slid a jumble of books to the side to make room for his elbow. It collapsed, sending a pile of student reports to the floor on the opposite side.

"Secondly," he said, "there is no Oscar #2, nor Lakshmi #2. There's only one of us—each. It's just that we're happening differently—and simultaneously—each of us."

"I'm clear on the science, thanks. I need a way to refer to the two— whatever. Trajectories. There's no word for it. And there's no word for the kind of fucked up my head is as a result. Look at this." She held her hand out. "I'm shaking—all the time. I never shook. We have to get a—"

"Wait, but I don't follow." He took a sip. "So does each version of us consider him/herself #1 and refer to the other as #2, or are we—this version of we, here—#2, like all the time, because it's not really fair having to be #2—all the time."

She stared back.

"OK. Whatever," he said. "But it's not fair."

Lakshmi tossed the bra on top of the fridge and cleared the empty grocery bags from a chair. She wrenched the back of Oscar's chair so he was turned toward her and pulled hers up to face him.

"Uh oh," he said.

Her eyes drifted from his and then darted about erratically. He watched until she refocused.

"What's going on, Lakki. You're freaking me out a little."

"I just came close—I should say, #1 just came close to rear-ending a garbage truck over on Maple."

"The hell. Sorry. Do you need to deal with that?"

She leaned back. "Is that what you're doing? Dealing with two lives at once?"

"It's one life actually."

"Shut up. Are you dealing with it? Because I'm not. I can't."

He lifted his glass. "I'm finding this helps."

She snatched his glass and put it on the table, then grabbed his wrists and yanked them to her.

"Hey, ow."

"Listen to me. And by that I mean Oscar #2 and #1. Listen." She yanked again.

"OK, OK. Both here."

She closed her eyes. "I need you to not be an asshole anymore. Because—"

Lakshmi's head jerked to the side and her eyes went wide. She shook herself and pulled Oscar's hands to her eyes.

"Hey, hey," he said. "What's wrong?"

She dropped his hands.

"OK, stupid question," he said. "But look, I was doomed from the start—asshole-wise. You needn't concern yourself. Join me. We'll drink ourselves free of this if it kills us." He reached for his glass.

She stood and left the room.

Oscar called after her. "I mean, really, you can dull the effects quite effectively with—"

He paused at the racket of households items tumbling out of the hall closet.

Lakshmi returned carrying a plastic mop bucket. She emptied the dry wash rags onto the floor, forced the bucket into the sink among the dishes and turned on the cold water tap.

"Think of it this way," he said. "If hypothetically we have a 50/50 chance of conviction for—well, whatever the prosecutor is dreaming up—our two versions give us double the odds that we'll be exonerated. Did I get that math right? I think living dueling lives has blunted my analytical instrument, or maybe it's this cheap vodka, and the cheap rye at McG's—and the cough syrup."

Lakshmi turned the tap off and lifted the bucket from the sink. She pivoted and dumped the contents over Oscar.

Oscar's sprung up, upsetting the table and sending clothes, dishes and papers flying. Lakshmi managed to grab him by the sweater before he fell. She leaned him against the counter, gripping his shoulders.

She shook him.

"Stop," he said. "Fuck."

She shook harder, then grabbed him by the ears.

"Shit. Why do they always go for the ears?"

"I don't care about you," she said. "You need to not be an asshole because you're the only one who understands what's happening to me. The hell if I'm going to go insane all by myself. I need help."

He waited for her to take a breath and then wrapped his hands around her fists to ease them loose.

"I don't know if I can help you, Lakshmi. I've always been—"

His eyes went dull.

He stood dripping for a moment, then wilted to the floor. "Oh, shit," he said and wrapped his arms around his knees.

Lakshmi stepped back. She righted a chair and sat.

Her leg was twitching. "I just need to be able to talk to somebody who understands," she said, "somebody not totally fucked up all the time. Can you keep your shit together that much for me?"

Oscar leaned back against the cabinet door, his eyes still unfocused.

She hugged herself and rocked. "Do you understand?" she said. "Tell me you understand."

He looked up. "Yes—not an asshole. Sorry. It's Micky. He just died."

McGonigel's was dead.

"Thanksgiving break?" replied Franky, as if questioning Oscar's mental health.

Oscar looked around. "Why are you even open on Thanksgiving?"

Franky slid Oscar his rye rocks. "Yesterday, kid. It was yesterday."

"Damn." He raised his glass. "Well, belated thanks."

Franky crossed his arms. "You weren't at the service."

"What?"

"Micky's funeral service. Otz would've liked you there."

"You know Otz?"

"Since back in the day."

"You've found him to be a reliable guy? True blue?" said Oscar.

"When the chips are down, yeah."

Oscar twirled his ice. "Kind of guy who'd leave his kid on his death bed and not come back? Kind of guy who'd leave a guy like me there to be with him when he died?"

"He did that?"

"Yup."

Franky rubbed his chin. "Maybe he couldn't handle being there."

"Maybe."

"Or maybe he thought it was more important for you to be there."

Oscar smirked. "Me? Micky's friend who spiked him with a tire iron and sent him to fiery hell? You think he wanted me to experience a life lesson?"

"As I understand it, what you did had something to do with Micky beating his friend to death," said Franky.

Oscar shrugged. "My friend, too."

He downed his drink and nodded to the bottle.

Franky measured out another shot. "I'm not one for offering advice, but here's what I think. You wanna know what I think about you and your situation?"

"What situation?"

"You saying you don't have a situation? Micky? Otz? This impossible science whatcha-ma-call?"

Oscar made a "bring-it-on" motion with his non-drinking hand.

"You need to understand the meaning of what respecting your fellow man means."

Oscar nodded. "Much obliged. Is that advice meant just for me or the collective scientific community?"

"I'd say start with just yourself, hotshot. That'd be a start. Start with yourself. To your own self be true."

Oscar drained his glass and smacked it down. He tapped the rim twice. "Thy."

"Yeah, thyself. And cut down on the sauce. You're gonna be dead before you get a chance." He reached over and poured Oscar another.

"You could be more of a suck-up to your only customer of the night."

Franky nodded toward the door.

Oscar kept his head down. "I was so enjoying our pillow talk."

Oscar watched the reflection in the bar mirror as the visitor passed behind him and took the next stool.

"What'll you have?" Franky asked him.

The guest pulled his sweatshirt hood down. "A pickled egg, please."

Oscar laughed. "I dig your new beard. It's manly, for a change."

Ranger turned to him. "I like my scarf."

Oscar tossed an end over his shoulder. "It's my fucking scarf now. You gave it to me just before you destroyed my fucking life, what was left of it."

"Yes," said Ranger. He unzipped his sweatshirt and chomped down his egg.

"Yes," he said again.

"And I lied. I think your beard looks like pubic hair." Oscar tapped twice on the bar. "Franky, one for my— well, for him, as well."

When the round arrived, Ranger lifted his glass and waited until Oscar complied.

"I'm sorry that I ruined your life," he said. "To friends."

Oscar grimaced. He clinked glasses and downed his shot. Ranger took a breath, squeezed his eyes tight and followed suit.

Oscar watched until Ranger was overcome with coughing. "First time?" He tapped twice on the bar.

"Yes," Ranger managed.

"Both of you's reached your limits," said Franky. He scooped up the glasses and put the rye back on the shelf.

Oscar and Ranger sat in silence for a good while, staring at the blinking pumpkin lights strung between the beer taps.

Oscar cleared his throat. "Ranger, we've got a situation." He avoided Franky's fatherly look.

"Wait," Oscar said, "why are you here? If I was you, I'd be in Thailand or where ever you go. Chile?"

"I was in Cooperstown."

"New York? Why the hell?"

"Hello," said Franky. "Baseball Hall of Fame."

Oscar stood and tapped Ranger on the shoulder. He headed for a booth in the back corner.

Ranger turned back and got two more eggs before joining Oscar.

"I must have driven there," Ranger said when he was done eating. "It's unclear. Much of that week remains unclear."

Oscar had a coaster set on edge. He attempted to rotate it like a top.

"How is Lakshmi?" said Ranger.

Oscar exhaled. "She's been cranky, and a bit of a nag, to be honest."

"You're present with her now?"

Oscar met his look. "Yeah. That's been a condition with respect to her nagginess, being with me a lot. I told her your beard is pubescent. She said she misses you."

"How many do you have?"

Oscar waited for more, then said. "Two. That what you mean? Both of us. Two."

"Yes, that's what I mean."

"You?" said Oscar.

Ranger closed his eyes and laid each of his fingers on the table, one at a time, then repeated the cycle, and then again. "Thirty-four, seems accurate."

Oscar's coaster rolled off the table. "Mother of God."

Ranger took a deep breath, folded his hands and exhaled through pursed lips. He repeated the exercise twice more.

"Originally, it was thirty-six," he said.

"What happened to the other two? Did you lose track of..."

Ranger was staring at him.

"Oh shit. You didn't."

"Closing up," Franky shouted. "Ten minutes."

Ranger looked at his hands. "It hasn't occurred to you? You—and Lakshmi as well—you would only have to do it once each."

"Fuck." Oscar leaned back. "I don't— Well, I guess I can see that, but—fuck."

"I thought I could keep going and carry out the act with all of them," Ranger said. "I told myself it was just—"

"Part of your process?"

Ranger watched Franky flipping stools onto the bar. "Essentially," he said. "I told myself I could distance myself. I thought I could treat it—academically. But—how can I say this?"

"Killing yourself 35 times takes a lot out of a guy?"

Ranger nodded. He stood.

"You didn't answer my question," said Oscar. "Why are you here?"

"I was getting to that." Ranger zipped up. "I have to make some arrangements tonight. I'll meet you at Lakshmi's apartment tomorrow morning, seven o'clock."

"Why? Kinda early for me."

"Be outside and ready to go. Pack enough for a week—both of you."

"You taking us to Cooperstown?"

He pulled his hood up. "Metaphorically speaking, perhaps, although I'm not clear on the metaphor."

Ranger turned and left.

Oscar sat on the stoop hugging his duffel bag, squinting through the glare of the early New England sun. He slid aside to make way for Lakshmi.

"Can you—?" She handed him her suitcase out the door and pulled two more bundles from the foyer.

"For a week? How many ratty sweatshirts do you need?"

She tossed the laundry bags onto the sidewalk. "Ranger told us a week to keep the baggage down. We're not coming back—at least, I know I'm not."

"How do you know that?"

She took her suitcase from him. "We chatted last night—him and me #3."

"What? Since when do you have a #3?"

"Since he taught #3 how to open up to #1 and #2."

They turned toward the noise at the intersection three blocks down.

"No way," said Oscar, as his old van came into view. "I'd know that squeal anywhere. I guess Otz's guy didn't replace that worn fan belt."

Micky barreled toward them, ignoring a stop sign. He made a U-turn across the double line and pulled up snug to the curb.

As if in a single motion, Micky hopped out and circled around to assist Lakshmi. He bowed deeply, stowed her bags through the back door, then tipped an invisible hat and held his palm out for a tip.

Oscar remained seated. Micky, continuing the mime routine, made a sad clown face, pacing, hands behind his back. He leaned against the van, crossed his arms and ankles, and raised an exaggerated eyebrow.

Tookie stepped down from the passenger's side and introduced himself to Lakshmi.

Ranger emerged from the back of the van. He approached Oscar.

"I thought you would understand," he said.

"Maybe I understand too well," Oscar said. "It's always been about the van for you."

"Yes."

"And you realize that's the last place I want to be again—ever—is in that van."

"All my memories from all my versions, they all go back to that night in the van," said Ranger. "Everything pivots on the van."

The wind was gusting. Oscar pulled his scarf up around his chin and stuck his hands between his knees. "And you think we can end it all in the van, too? We can end our situation?"

"Not end. We can complete the circle. But first I need to teach you all to open up."

Oscar looked at Micky and Tookie, cutting it up with Lakshmi. "All of us? But those numbskulls weren't there with Lakshmi and us. They didn't take part in the experiment."

"Not necessary. I can teach them."

"That would suggest you can teach any damn body."

"Maybe. Yes."

The threesome by the van wound down their antics and looked Oscar's way.

Oscar stood and hung the duffel on his shoulder. He looked up the boulevard, then turned to look the other way.

He descended the stairs, stood for a moment, and then stepped toward the van.

Micky bounded the remaining distance and snatched the duffel. "We, my fine friend, are on a mission, and the mother-frigging mission begins now."

Oscar pointed at him. "You're not driving, Mr. Human Torch. And the hell if I'm driving because—well, it's too painful to my psyche. And Ranger's negotiating space in thirty-four iterations, so no way we're letting him drive. So that leaves you, Took, or Lakshmi, maybe, if she can keep her shit intact."

The group exchanged looks.

"Deal," said Micky.

"As long as I don't have to cozy up next to art man," said Tookie, and headed for the driver side.

They climbed in, Ranger, Lakshmi and Oscar taking their places on the newly-installed bench seat in the back. Micky hopped into the front passenger seat and bounced like a sugar-buzzed child. He beat out a rhythm on the dash and worked it into a drum roll.

Oscar scooched down in his seat and wrapped his scarf around his face.

Tookie started the engine.

"Micky?" said Lakshmi.

Micky paused his racket and turned to her. "Yes, sister? How can I help you?" He made a sign of benediction.

"What is our mission?"

He glanced at Ranger. "Why, isn't it obvious? We are the agents of change. We're gonna teach the universe to be self-aware and, in so doing, free humankind from the oppressive boundaries of our wretched, singular existences. Are you down with that?"

"Yes, very much so." Lakshmi put an arm around Oscar's shoulder and pressed her cheek to his scalp.

Tookie wrenched the column shifter into drive and pealed out from the curb.

"Where to?" asked Lakshmi.

"Sorry sister," said Mickey above the engine noise. "You'll need to speak up."

Lakshmi let it fly. "Hey! What's our designation?"

"Cooperstown!" they shouted in unison.

Addendum

THE CATERPILLAR'S TOMB

By ®Anger

Oh! meat locker cold,
Quake me with stingless shivers,
Tickle these nostril-caves,
With tinkling stalactites, icy follicles,
Mocking these breathless lungs,
Going whispy-clink, the air through my nostricles.

Blanketed lit-less city night,
Paint these woozy streets with orangy-gray light.
Muffle the cries of the dull–lit–city,
As my breath-billows reach for the windshield night.

Cold worries down the Oscar-clouds' rising.
Outside, voice-clatter, all kit-a-braah.
Braaaah. "Fucker, you." Rat-a-braah.
Crackling boots circle, whetstone grinding.

To fit, I sit,
Where in murky van shadows,
Oscar curls frozen,
In a mildew-frosted shroud.
A gas can fumes,
And from beyond, tuned sharp and loud,
The killer's bar,
Sings for entry to the caterpillar's tomb.

Beneath Oscar's eye, the thin, gentle fold,
Guides the salty trail,
And with rat-abraah chiseling our frozen ears,
Clink for clank, pound for pound,
The iron, a mace on armor pinging,
Has its way with the growl-gulped moaner.
The iron, once sated, falls weighted, ringing.

Searchy-key, scratchy.
Caterpillar-Oscar, ball tight!
There now, dead Tookie fits,
His ropy arms flail rubbery adangle,
His gummy frozen blacky-blood and eye-pooly,
Over-woven by a tarred snake tangle.

The steam killer's weapon, friends,
Let me tell you,
It's a tire bar.
It's an iron fire bar.
It's an iron in the fire.
It's a tire iron, friends, a tire iron.

Oscar hissing 'neath the rumbly, stands,
Grasping the iron with numbly flipifers.
As tires grind the road-ice-crunchy,
Steam Killer shrieks like a widow, pounding,
Beats the wheel, double-fisted,
Pounding, pounding the piteous wheel.

Rocking and wailing across lanes,
Punching the van past streaking glinties,
Past diamond-strung street lamps,
The killer is mesmerized into squinties.
Then Oscar, up,
Swing-falls left, puncturing the killer's dream,
Freeing the inky stream,
Loosing the unspeakable scream.

It's happening now, Oscar.
"It's now!"

The first car kisses them,

The second misses them,

The third bites them, spins them,

The fourth ignites them,

The fifth suspends them,

Then, once re-grounded,

The fifth one ends them.

About the author :

Rick Moss is a multi-disciplinary artist living in Brooklyn, New York. He earned his degree in fine arts and devoted a good portion of his career to design—print, video, and web. He is a founding principle of the online business forum, RetailWire, where he oversees editorial and marketing content. He publishes his songwriting as Rock Moses.

Ebocloud (2013), his first novel, published by Aqueous Books, is a near-future thriller about a massive social media movement.

His second, *Tellers* (2016), stitched together a series of short stories with an overarching narrative thread.